TOMB OF TREASURE

SCHOLASTIC

Scholastic Children's Books,
Euston House, 24 Eversholt Street,
London, NW1 1DB, UK

A division of Scholastic Ltd
London ~ New York ~ Toronto ~ Sydney ~ Auckland
Mexico City ~ New Delhi ~ Hong Kong

Published in the UK by Scholastic Ltd, 2008

Text copyright © Terry Deary, 2008
Illustrations copyright © Martin Brown, Mike Phillips, 2008
All rights reserved

ISBN 978 1407 10296 2

Printed and bound by Bookmarque Ltd, Croydon, Surrey

4 6 8 10 9 7 5 3

The right of Terry Deary, Martin Brown and Mike Phillips to be identified as the author and illustrator of this work respectively has been asserted by them in accordance with the Copyright, Designs and Patents Act, 1988.

This book is sold subject to the condition that it shall not, by way of trade or otherwise be lent, resold, hired out, or otherwise circulated without the publisher's prior consent in any form of binding or cover other than that in which it is published and without a similar condition, including this condition, being imposed on a subsequent purchaser.

Papers used by Scholastic Children's Books are made from wood grown in sustainable forests.

GORY STORIES

TOMB OF TREASURE

TERRY DEARY

ILLUSTRATED BY MARTIN BROWN

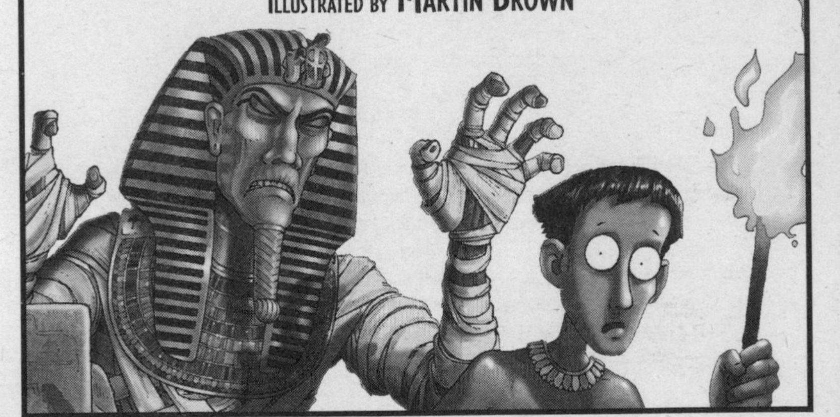

INTRODUCTION

Do NOT read this book!
You have been warned!!
It is horrible!!!
Why are you still reading?

All right ... let me put it another way. Only read this book if you have nerves as strong as scaffolding poles. Only read on if you laugh at nightmares and can kill the monsters under your bed with a slap of your slipper. Only read this book if you are tough enough to look in a history teacher's dirty-washing basket and not turn pale and throw up.

In other words, only read this book if you are a superhero like Spider-Bat Boy or Wonder-Worm Woman ... or me.

For I have looked into the darkest and dirtiest, most miserable and murkiest corners of history. I've uncovered a tale so shocking it turned my hair white with fright. White as a snowman's bum in fact.

Not that you'll find any snowmen in this tale. The only snowman you'd see in ancient Egypt would have been a suicide-snowman.

There is an ancient legend that says a brave snowman once crossed the Sahara Desert. He travelled in a fridge on wheels. I don't believe this story. You have to ask, 'Where did he plug it in?'

It was hot and dry, dusty and dangerous.

I have been there so you don't have to. (You'll be pleased to hear this – especially if you're a snowman.)

Let me take you back to Egypt in the year 1327 BC.

The kings of Egypt were gods … or so they believed. When they died they were buried with more riches than a poor worker could earn in a hundred lifetimes.

So it's no wonder those poor Egyptians hungered for the gold. No wonder that they set up secret robber gangs to pillage the pyramids and grab from the graves.

The punishments for being caught were terrible. There were some very hungry crocodiles in the River Nile waiting to eat the bits of you that the grave guards threw in … get the picture?

The grave builders tried to make the tombs thief-proof. Yet still the robbers won the battle of wits.

A 'battle of wits' is the struggle between the minds of the grave builders and the minds of the robbers. This is not at all like the struggle between two footballers – that is a 'battle of twits'.

By 1900 every single royal grave in Egypt had been emptied. Clean as a whistle in a washing machine. The ones the robbers missed were robbed by the museums.

Well … every grave that was known about. There are just a few graves that everyone had missed. One was that of a forgotten pharaoh that had stayed hidden for 3,000 years.

The grave of the boy-king Tutankhamun.

In 1922 a team of diggers finally unearthed King Tut's tomb in the Valley of the Kings. So now we could see exactly how a pharaoh was buried. At last we could look into a tomb that hadn't been emptied by robbers. Tutankhamun went from being forgotten to being famous.

The diggers sent Tut on a journey round the world – a great and golden show. How would YOU like to be dug up thousands of years after you die to be stared at by strangers? Creepy, eh? Tut and all his secrets went on show.

There were stories that said Tut didn't much like being disturbed. He had been protected by a curse. That curse came back to haunt the diggers and killed them one by one!

Haunted horsefeathers. Phantom flim-flam. Spectral silliness. And ghostly gobbledygook. There is no Curse of Tutankhamun.

But there IS still a mystery about that tomb. When the 1922 diggers finally reached the door to the tomb they found it had been damaged and repaired in two places.

So Tutankhamun's tomb HAD been robbed – yet not much had been taken. Why? How? What is the story behind it? Who were the robbers?

We will never know all the answers. But there were clues left behind, so we can guess.

We can go back 3,000 years and follow a team of tomb-robbers through that dreadful day when they tried to take Tutankhamun's treasure.

Their story could almost be true...

SHADOWS, SOLDIERS AND SCUM

The water-clock dripped towards noon as fat Maiarch sat on the mud bench and sipped the cool, sweet beer. She pulled a face.

'Antef!' she spat. 'This beer has more bits in it than the desert has grains of sand!'

The old man grinned and showed his black and yellow stumps of teeth.

It was the bread. Egyptians ground the corn with stones and bits of stone got in the bread. So the bread ground their teeth. Stick some sand in your bread and what do you get? A real sand-wich! Hoh! Hoh! Hoh! Oh, all right, it wasn't THAT funny.

'At least you haven't any teeth to get the bits stuck in!' he said cheerfully.

She tried to snarl. It's hard to do a good snarl when you pull back your lips and only show your pale pink gums. 'Why are we drinking this mud?' she asked.

Antef spread his hard, wrinkled hands. 'I'll get you a cup of Nile water if you want a drink.'

Maiarch clutched her wrinkled throat. 'I may be old but I don't want to die just yet.'

Antef's dark eyes glittered in the cool gloom. 'I'll find some river water with some tasty crocodile dung ... or would you rather have hippo droppings?' He leaned forward and Maiarch could see the scars of a hundred lashings on his creased brown back.

The old woman sipped her cloudy beer. 'They should

be here by now,' she grumbled. 'I hope they haven't been caught by the King's guards.'

Antef snorted. 'Why would the King's guards arrest our friends? They haven't done anything!'

'No ... but they're going to! They're going to plot the greatest robbery in history,' the woman argued.

'The guards don't know that,' Antef sighed.

Maiarch jabbed a fat finger at him. 'Of course they know! They know you are a cheap thief...'

'I am a master thief ... lord of the thieves! No one has stolen as much from the rich as I have,' he crowed.

'And no one has been caught and whipped so often,' she snorted. 'General Menes said next time you're caught he'll have you executed ... very slowly.'

'I have been biding my time. Waiting for the one great crime. A crime fit for a man who is the greatest thief the world has ever seen!'

'You are the greatest scum the Nile has ever seen – why, you would steal your own mother's eyes if you could sell them!'

'My mother's dead!'

'That wouldn't stop you!'

'I meant...'

'I know what you meant. You meant they don't know you are plotting to rob the King's tomb.'

Antef opened his mouth to speak but Maiarch went on, 'Of course they know you will try. And you sit here, sipping filthy beer and you think you are so-o clever.'

'In seventy days we will be sitting on golden thrones, sipping wine!' Antef chuckled.

'Seventy days from now we will not be sitting on golden thrones. Seventy days from now we will be lucky to be alive,' Maiarch grumbled.

'So why are you here? Why are you here before the others?' Antef chuckled.

The woman sighed. 'Because you might … for once in your miserable life … you just might succeed.'

'Succeed in what?' came a quiet voice from the doorway.

Antef squawked. Maiarch gasped.

'Where did you come from?' the old man demanded.

The skinny boy stepped forward. 'I slipped in behind the curtain.'

'I never saw the curtain move,' Antef said angrily. 'You must be as slippery as a catfish.'

'It's my job.'

'Your job?'

'House thief,' the boy said softly. He was balanced on his toes, ready to spring away – more like a cat than a catfish.

Antef smiled and patted the mud bench beside him. 'You must be the famous Paneb. Sit here.'

'Famous?' the boy squeaked softly. 'I'm not famous. I've never been caught or punished.'

'You are famous in the taverns and the underworld of Thebes,' Antef said.

The boy squatted carefully on the seat beside the old man. He wrinkled his nose a little at the ancient smell of sour sweat, stale beer and old onions.

He'd smell of onions and beer because that's what peasants ate and drank. He'd smell of stale sweat because he never bathed. Imagine if YOU had a story written about you and the writer said YOU smelled of stale sweat. You'd be so ashamed. Go and have a bath right now or it may just happen.

'When you have worked with Antef you will be one of the most fabulous five thieves in Thebes,' Antef said.

The old woman shook with silent laughter. 'Or you will be in five fabulous pieces floating down the Nile for a crocodile's breakfast.'

The boy swallowed hard. 'What do you want me to do?'

'Help us rob the tomb of King Tutankhamun,' Antef said simply.

The boy nodded. His wide eyes looked too large for his thin face. 'I see.' He looked at the old man. 'How will we do it?'

'With the help of two more friends who are coming to join us,' Antef told him.

The boy's wide ears caught the sound of sandals on the stony path outside the house. The curtain was brushed aside and for a moment the sunlight flooded in. Then the light was blocked by the massive shadow of the man in the doorway. His shoulders brushed each side of the door and he had to duck his large, square head to peer inside.

The stranger asked and his deep voice made the mud walls shake.

'It's a secret,' Antef snapped. 'Nobody knows about it.'

'*I* know about it. You told my brother to tell me to come. I'm Big Neria.'

'Then what is the password?' Antef asked.

'Pass-what?'

'Password? You have to give the right answer to *prove* you are not from the King's guard.'

The big man shook his shaved head. 'The king's guard wouldn't have me as a soldier. I asked to join. They said I was too stupid.' He frowned and looked at the dusty floor. 'That's not a very nice thing to say,' he muttered. 'How would you like it if a captain of the guard called *you* stupid?'

'I wouldn't like it at all,' Antef said shaking his head.

'That's why I picked up his club and cracked him over the head,' Big Neria said.

'Did it do a lot of damage?' Paneb said in a small voice.

'Oh yes! The club split in three pieces!' Neria said. 'Anyway. I've come to the secret meeting.'

'Password?' fat Maiarch hissed.

Big Neria rubbed his chin. 'Give me a clue.'

'I say something and you have to give the right answer,' Antef explained.

'All right,' Big Neria said and his square face crumpled in thought.

'The ... King ... is ... dead,' Antef said.

'*I* know. I heard that in the tavern,' Big Neria nodded. 'Some people reckon his uncle Ay had something to do with it. *Mur*-der!'

Antef blew out his cheeks and supped some warm beer. 'That is my half of the password. You have to give the right reply,' he said.

'Oh, I see. Try again,' Big Neria grinned.

'The ... King ... is ... dead.'

'Dead as a duck's toenail ... at least that's what they said in the tavern.' The big man smiled.

Old Antef grated his teeth stumps and said loudly, 'The ... King ... is ... dead. That's the password. I say it and you say, "Long live the King!" Understand?'

'If the King's dead then how can he long live?' Big Neria grunted.

'Tutankhamun is dead ... but Ay will take the throne. So we have a new king. Tutankhamun is dead ... long live King Ay, is what it means.'

'I see! Glad that's settled. Now, what's the secret plot?'

'We are waiting for one more member of the Fabulous Five,' Antef sighed.

Big Neria sat on a mud bench just as the curtain swung back and a man as tall as Neria looked in. Antef gave a choked cry while Maiarch sucked air through her wrinkled gums. Young Paneb shrank so small he seemed just a shadow in the gloomy room ready to slide away like a catfish.

'The King is dead!' Big Neria cried happily.

'Long live the King,' the stranger said smoothly. His body was hard and golden as brass. His face had more sharp angles than a pyramid but it was a handsome and clever face.

'Welcome to the Fabulous Five,' Neria said and rose to greet the newcomer. 'I'm Neria, but I just arrived. I don't know who the others are yet.'

'I think I can help you,' the stranger said. 'Antef over there is the biggest rogue in Thebes. Fat Maiarch is as twisted as a serpent. The boy is probably the house thief we haven't caught. And you are Neria the Stupid, who goes around cracking clubs over my guard captains.'

'*Your* captains?' Neria scowled.

'My captains,' the man said softly.

Antef groaned. 'Stupid, stupid, Neria ... this is General Menes ... head of the palace guard.'

The smile slipped off Neria's face like a crocodile over wet mud.

'Oh dear,' he said. 'Oh dear, oh dear.'

Do you want to be a writer? Some people do. If you do then note how this chapter ends. The reader asks, 'How on EARTH will they get out of that?' You will have to read on to find out. In fact so will I. A lot of writers know where their story is going. I haven't a clue. If you don't mind I'll join you in the next chapter to find out...

Funerals, Five and Fabulous

General Menes stepped into the centre of the room. His nose wrinkled at the sharp smell of Antef's dirt-crusted feet.

'The King is dead…' he began.

'Long live the King!' Big Neria cried. 'Sorry, General,' he muttered.

'The King is dead,' the guard repeated. 'It will take seventy days for his mummy to be completed. Then he will be buried with all his wealth.'

'We know…' Big Neria began. Maiarch hissed at him sharply and he shut his mouth with a snap.

'A king needs his wealth so he can live in comfort in the next life,' General Menes explained. 'Some villains in Thebes seem to think the gold would help them to live in comfort in this life. They will try to rob King Tutankhamun's grave.'

'That's shocking,' Antef whined. 'Who would dream of doing a thing like that?'

The General glared at him. His eyes narrowed. 'It is my job to stop them.'

Everyone looked nervous. Even Big Neria. 'What will happen if we get caught?' he asked. His huge fists were tight and the knuckles white, and his thick eyebrows met in the middle with a scowl that would scare a desert lion.

Antef jumped to his feet. 'He didn't mean that! He didn't mean to say if WE get caught because we aren't planning such a horrible crime. No ... Big *stupid* Neria meant what would happen if THEY get caught ... these grave-robbers you are out to catch.'

Menes took the club that hung from his belt – a fine club with a smooth lump of granite rock on the end. He slapped it into the palm of his other hand. 'What will happen, camel-brain?' he asked. 'The new king "Ay" will have you crucified – nailed to the walls of Thebes city. He will show the world what happens to grave-robbers.' He slapped the club firmly into his palm. 'And I will hammer in the nails myself. I will make a mud bench on the path by the wall and sit there to watch you die ... slowly.'

'Oh,' Neria muttered and swallowed hard. Paneb shifted on the cool earth seat and shivered.

'But we won't be caught,' Antef said smoothly, 'because we don't plan to rob anyone.'

The General stretched out the club and placed the stone tip under Antef's chin. He smiled. 'I will be happy to see my King buried peacefully.'

'So will we.' Maiarch nodded.

Menes shrugged. 'I will be happy to crucify you on the walls of Thebes and watch you die slowly.' His voice dropped to a murmur. 'But happiest of all I would like to bury Tutankhamun safely AND catch you trying to rob him. Then I get BOTH of my wishes.'

The only sound was the gurgling of Antef's stomach as his onions shifted around with fear.

Does that ever happen to you? Your tummy rumbles JUST when everything is quiet. Everyone looks at you and you feel so-o embarrassed. Just as teacher is telling you off... 'Did you copy this homework from Jack?' Before you can answer your stomach does it for you ... 'rumble, rumble, rumble'.

Menes smiled a nasty smile. 'So go on, Antef. Go ahead, make my day. Plan your robbery. You have seventy days.'

He turned to leave. He stopped and looked back. 'Five?'

'Five?' Antef asked.

'Neria said there were five of you. I can only count four,' the General growled.

'Ah!' Antef laughed nervously. 'I can see you put your abacus to good use in school. You learned how to count.'

General Menes stepped forward. He raised the club slightly. 'Five. Who is the fifth?'

Fat Maiarch pushed herself to her feet and her face wobbled into a sly look. 'Big Neria had just joined us … to share a jar of beer. He thought you were a fifth person come to the party.'

'Party?'

'Funeral party … we were drinking to the memory of good King Tutankhamun.' She smiled and showed her gums.

'I will be watching you,' the General said.

Maiarch nodded happily. 'I know … many men have watched me. They cannot take their eyes away from my beautiful face.' Her lips were coloured with red lip-tint and they showed bright against her pink gums. The sight made even General Menes shudder.

Menes did not smile. 'Plan your robbery.'

'What robbery?' Maiarch asked and blew a kiss at him. He ignored her and looked at Antef.

'Plan your robbery … please plan your robbery. Make my day.'

He turned and ducked through the doorway.

The four thieves let out their breath together as if they'd all been holding it in since the guard had entered.

Big Neria sighed. 'So it looks as if the robbery is off.'

'The grave of every King of Egypt has been robbed,' Antef said. 'But the clever robbers don't wait till after the funeral. They plan it before the king is put in his tomb. That's the best way to do it. I should know. We have seventy days.'

I think you've got the message. Seventy days. Ah, but WHY seventy days? Why not just dump old Tut's corpse in the cave and cover it up? Because it took seventy days for the mummy-salt - 'natron' - to suck up all the body juices and dry him out. Try it for yourself the next time you find a dead teacher in your classroom.

'Seventy days to outwit General Menes,' Maiarch nodded. 'Should be easy enough. He's only a soldier. One woman is worth ten soldiers like him.'

'And we have TWO women,' Antef laughed. He looked towards the door where a shadowy figure could be seen through the curtain. 'Come in, young Dalifa,' Antef cried.

The curtain slid back and a girl hurried in.

Little Paneb looked at her and stepped back. The girl's hair was curled into ringlets and tied with flax. She had shaded her eyes with green and black colouring. She wore more lip-tint than Maiarch. It didn't make her look any prettier – her face was thin and her nose as sharp as a knife blade. Paneb made a face as if he'd sucked on Antef's onions. 'It's not a woman ... it's just a girl!'

The girl's wide brown eyes glowed with rage. 'Just? What do you mean, just? You are skinny as a sparrow's leg and I could snap you in two just as easily,' she raged and stepped towards him. Paneb rose to face her. The girl was his height but better-fed and heavier. Antef stepped between them.

'Stop, Dalifa!' he ordered. 'Save your strength for the seventy days ahead. We cannot fight among ourselves.'

'Fight? Fight? It wouldn't be much of a fight. I would

break Twig-boy in two. Then I'd crush him under my heel, then I'd take a brush and sweep him into the Nile. The poor crocodiles wouldn't find enough flesh to make a meal of him.'

'I said stop!' old Antef ordered. 'We are a team. The Fabulous Five of Thebes. Together we can be the Richest Five of Thebes. We each have our place in the team.'

Dalifa made a 'pah' noise with her lips. 'I suppose the boy's place is fetching beer and cleaning the toilet pit.'

'He has an important part to play. As important as you,' Antef said quietly.

'But I don't have to *like* Twig-boy,' the girl spat.

'You do NOT have to like him, but you DO have to trust him,' Maiarch said gently. 'Can you do that, Dalifa?'

The girl glared, gave a sharp nod and sat on a bench. The ribbons were battling to control her dark hair. The ribbons were losing the battle. Dalifa glared across the room at little Paneb before she turned to Antef. 'So what is the plan, master thief?'

Antef was happy. He had four people listening to his every word. He began. 'When we die we go to the afterlife,' Antef reminded them.

'What? Even if we are nailed to the walls of Thebes?' Neria asked.

'Shut up,' Dalifa told him.

'Sorry, I'm sure,' the man mumbled.

'The spirit leaves the body,' Antef went on. 'It wanders the dark pathways and corridors of the underworld until it finds the place it is looking for.'

'The Hall of Judgement – the Hall of Osiris – where

our spirits will be judged,' Paneb breathed.

'At each step of the journey there is danger!' Antef warned. 'Vicious doorkeepers who only let you pass if you know your name.'

'Easy! I'm Paneb,' the boy said.

Dalifa looked at him with scorn. 'But will you remember that after you die, Twig-boy?'

'Yes.' He said. 'I will have "The Book of the Dead" with me. It will tell me all I need to know – my name, the names of the doorkeepers – even the names of the door bolts and the floorboards!'

'Hah!' she sneered. 'But when your heart is weighed against a feather will it pass the test?'

'Yes!' he said fiercely.

The girl leaned across and looked into his eyes. 'Ammit is waiting for you.'

'I know,' the boy mumbled and he shuffled as if he was sitting on a scarab beetle.

'Ammit has the head of a crocodile, the front body of a lion and the backside of a hippo,' Dalifa said sweetly. 'When your wicked heart is weighed against a feather she is waiting. Waiting to see if your sins have made the heart too heavy.'

Paneb's mouth was dry. He wanted to say, 'I know,' but the words stuck in his throat.

Dalifa smiled. 'Do you know what will happen to your heart if it fails the test?' she went on.

Paneb said nothing.

'Ammit will use her crocodile mouth to chew it up and swallow it. Then you will be barred from the afterlife. For all time, you will have to die and die again and again and...'

EEK!

'Stop tormenting the boy,' Old Antef ordered.

'He said I was *just* a girl,' Dalifa reminded him. 'Well Ammit is just a girl too ... waiting to swallow him if he ever calls me just a girl again!' she snapped.

'You're scaring the boy,' Maiarch said gently.

'No! I am just reminding him how careful he has to be. One mistake and he doesn't just lose this life – he loses any chance of reaching heaven in the afterlife,' Dalifa spat.

Big Neria said, 'We'll just have to make sure we don't get caught, then!'

Maiarch looked at him with surprise. 'Neria! That is a very sensible thing to say!'

The big man grinned. 'Thanks!'

'You are not as stupid as you look.'

His face fell. 'Thanks.'

When I say his face 'fell' I don't mean it dropped off and fell on the floor. That would be messy. It's one of those strange things writers say when they mean something else. 'Face fell' means he was 'disappointed'. So why couldn't I just say that in the first place? Good question. YOU aren't as stupid as you look either!

NERIA, NATRON AND KNIVES

Two men left the town of Thebes and walked towards the dusty desert in the east. A warm wind whirled sand around them and they covered their faces with scarves. The path was rocky and as they came near a boulder the big man pulled out a black, stone knife and checked it was safe to walk past.

'It's all right, Antef!' he called. 'Not a desert lion in sight.'

'Or a jackal? A hungry jackal will attack a traveller too, you know, Neria.'

'No jackals. Not even a cat!' Neria told the old man.

Antef scuttled past the boulder nervously. 'I wish we could see a cat! It's lucky if you see a cat,' he explained.

'There are always cats in the House of Death!' Neria said, excited.

Antef sighed. 'They are *dead* cats. They don't count. They kill them and turn them into mummies to bring the king luck in the next life. Oh yes, Neria, take my word for it. Cats are lucky.'

Neria thought about it. 'Not so lucky for the cats though. I mean ... they get killed so they can keep the dead king company! That's not lucky!'

Antef shrugged. 'Better than the old pharaohs,' Antef said with a harsh laugh. 'They didn't kill cats for company ... they killed their servants!'

'They didn't!'

'They did. Think of it. You served your pharaoh faithfully for fifty years. He dies – and you get smashed on the head so you can join him in his pyramid. *That's* bad luck for you.'

'What's a pyramid?' Neria asked.

Antef stopped, took Neria's knife and scratched in the road dust a large triangle.

People often ask, 'What is the point of a pyramid?' and I always tell them, 'It's the sharp bit at the top!' They never laugh. Maybe they don't get the joke. Maybe they don't see the point.

'What's that?' Neria asked.

'A pyramid,' Antef said. 'I saw those when I went north to fight the Hyskos! When I was young I was the greatest warrior in Egypt ... well, the greatest warrior in our village ... well, I was the *only* warrior in our village. But I was brave. They marched us north and that's when I first saw the ancient pyramids,' he explained and jabbed the knife at the shape on the ground.

'What are they?' Neria asked.

'They are huge stone piles that reach up into the clouds. They used to bury the dead kings in them in the old days,' Antef said. 'At least that's what I was told. Up in the north, near Gaza, there are nearly a hundred of these tombs. Each one took years to build and thousands of farmers worked on them when it was too dry to work in the fields. You should go and see them one day, Neria,' Paneb said. 'They are a wonder.'

'I bet no one could get in to rob one of those,' Neria said.

Antef snorted. 'Well you'd be wrong, young man. They've all been robbed. Oh, they built secret passages and hidden entrances. They put traps and pits in the dark corridors – darker than the underworld – but the robbers still got in. They're all empty now.'

'But how did they get in?' the big man asked.

Antef patted Neria's knee. 'They robbed the tomb before the king was ever buried there.'

'They were as crafty as you,' Neria chuckled.

'One king, Cheops, tried to bury his mother in a pit as deep as six tall men,' Antef cried. 'It was filled with jewelled chests, silver statues and golden furniture. She was called Queen Heterpheres. Then Cheops died a happy man – he was sure his mother and her treasure were safe from the robbers. Hah!' he cackled. 'If anyone ever bothers to dig down they'll find it empty.'

'Grave-robbers?' Neria breathed and dreamed of the riches.

'On our way home from the wars,' Antef said to Neria, 'my captain took me to the pyramid of Cheops. The secret entrance had been found a thousand years ago. But it was sealed with great granite blocks.'

'You can't dig through granite,' the big man said.

Antef winked. 'No, young man. So we saw the place where the robbers had dug *around* the blocks. We followed the passages to the centre of the tomb.'

'What did you find?' Neria gasped.

'We found the great pyramid had three rooms – one for King Cheops, one for his queen and perhaps one for his treasure,' he said.

'Did you find the treasure?' Neria asked.

Antef gave a grim smile. 'There was no treasure, only a huge stone coffin in the King's chamber.'

'The mummy.' Neria nodded. 'They'd have put some treasure in the mummy's coffin.'

Antef looked at him. 'We lifted the lid on the coffin, and there it was!'

'What was?'

Antef took a deep breath and said, 'Nothing!'

'Nothing!' Neria groaned, disappointed.

'Nothing. The coffin was empty.'

'I suppose the mummy had got out and walked off to

the afterlife, had he?'

Antef spread his hands. 'Who knows? Maybe Cheops died before the pyramid was finished and they had to bury him somewhere else. Or maybe the pyramid was never meant to be his resting place. It's a mystery as old as time.

And, two thousand years after Antef's day it's STILL a mystery. Lots of clever people have lots of clever ideas but no one really knows. Where is the missing mummy? If you find it then take it home – it's probably looking for its daddy! Hah! Yes, all right, another terrible joke.

'But I'll never forget my visit to the heart of Cheops' pyramid.' He leaned forward and said softly, 'I've heard it said that the pyramid was never meant to be a tomb!'

'I thought you said it was!'

Antef gave a clever smirk on his face. 'Some say it was built by the priests to measure time or study the stars.'

He took a date from a pocket in his tunic, chewed on it and spat out the stone. 'When we are rich we can spend all night studying the stars because we won't have to work. Let's rob Tutankhamun's tomb then other fools can worry about empty pyramids,' he said fiercely. 'Now let's get to the House of Death.'

The two men wrapped their scarves around their mouths and set off again.

The House of Death wasn't a house.

A House of Death isn't a house. A pack of wolves isn't a pack of cards. You wouldn't mop a floor with a mop of hair. Dog food isn't made out of dead dogs any more than angel cake is made out of dead angels. Words are a bigger mystery than Tutankhamun's grave.

It was a tent.

No, it wasn't a tent ... because tents have sides and the House of Death was just a cotton roof held up with poles. The roof kept the burning sun off the workers inside but let the wind blow the smell of death away: the smell of dead cats and rotting human remains.

The jackals and the desert lions hadn't bothered Neria and Antef on the path. That was because the jackals and the desert lions were gathered round where the wind blew the scent of death. They were waiting for a nibble, a snack or even a massive munching meal. A king's corpse would be nice ... desert lions can be snobby. They seem to think a king tastes better than a peasant like you or me. This is good news for you but bad news for kings, queens and the rest of the royal family.

Of course that was why the House of Death (which wasn't a house) was guarded by soldiers with spears, clubs and bows and arrows. A big golden cat could rush in looking like a desert lion ... then be carried away looking like a porcupine, it had so many arrows in its big golden body.

The guards could keep away the lions – they couldn't keep away the flies or the smell.

Antef walked up to the first guard. He was fat, flabby and fearful of the strangers. Big Neria looked terrifying.

'Password!' he squeaked.

'I am Antef of Thebes and I have brought a new worker for the House of Death.'

'Hello!' Neria said cheerfully.

'But do you know the password?' the guard asked.
'Of course *I* do,' Antef laughed. 'I bet you don't.'
'I do!'
'No you don't!!' the old man jeered. 'General Menes is a friend of mine. He came to my house this afternoon, didn't he, Neria?'
'He did,' the big man boomed. 'He threatened to nail us to...'
'And General Menes told us,' Antef cut in quickly. 'General Menes said you guards are hopeless. He said you always forget which password it is each day!'
The tubby guard tapped his chest with a chubby finger.
'I know it.'
'Pshaw!' Antef snorted. 'If you *know* it then what is it?'
'Nefertiti!' the guard announced proudly.
Antef beamed and his black teeth glittered. 'Well done that man! I will tell General Menes what a great guard you are. What's your name?'
'Thekel, sir,' the guard said, pushing his chest out and lifting his chin proudly.
'General Menes shall hear about you, Thekel. Well done. Well done.' The old man patted the blushing guard on the arm and walked past into the shade of the House of Death.
He walked boldly up to a man who carried a mask under his arm. It was the sharp-nosed head of a jackal. 'Are you the priest of Anubis?'
The man had a shaved head and his big ears stood out

like handles on a wine jar. 'Who are you?' he asked and peered closely at Antef's filthy clothes and even filthier feet. 'If you want me to turn you into a mummy you have to be dead first. Want me to call a guard and arrange it?'

Antef knew just how to deal with people like him.

'You should be wearing that mask. If the high priest Nesumontu saw you wandering around with the mask under your arm, he would have you whipped.'

'Who'd tell him?' the red-faced man demanded.

'I will when I see him tonight. He's a good friend of mine, you know.'

The Priest of Anubis looked unsure. 'It's hot wearing the mask all the time.'

'It will be hotter if Nesumontu has you staked out in the desert in the midday sun and lets the scorpions crawl all over you.'

'He wouldn't...'

'No ... he wouldn't!' Antef said with a sudden smile. 'Because I am not going to tell him!'

'You're not? Why not?'

'Because you are going to look after my nephew Neria here,' the old man said, waving a hand at his big friend. 'Look after him well and I will not breathe a word to Nesumontu ... look after him really well and I will see you are well rewarded by King Ay.'

'Ay?'

'Aye ... I will. Neria has been sent to help with the mummy-making. Train him well – he's a strong lad and he will be useful.'

The priest smiled weakly. 'I'll do my best,' he said.

'He can stay here tonight and start work tomorrow – Tutankhamun will be delivered tomorrow, I expect?'

'Yes, sir,' the priest said.

'Good.' Antef nodded. He took Neria by the arm and led him to the edge of the tent. 'There you are, my boy. Part one of the plan complete. We have a member of the fabulous five in the House of Death itself.'

'Who?' Neria asked.

Antef rolled his eyes and wondered if this was such a good idea. 'You, Neria. You are our inside man. Sixty-nine more days and you'll be rich.'

'Ooooh!' Neria said. 'Good!'

The Priest of Anubis walked up to Neria. 'You can start tomorrow on the body of an old scribe.'

'What do you want me to do?'

'Remove the brain ... tomorrow I'll show you how to take out a human brain,' the priest promised. 'I may even show you how to take out the guts.'

'Nice,' Neria said ... but he didn't look too sure. He stared out over the desert and watched Antef walk back to the city. The setting sun blazed golden red like the fires of the underworld. The fires that would burn the fabulous five if they failed.

Neria shivered.

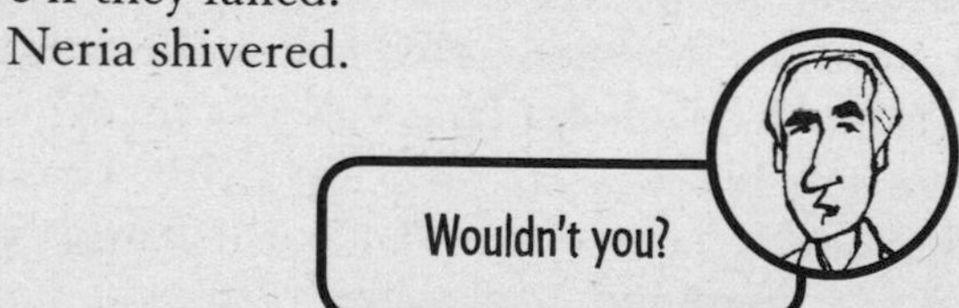

GOATS, GLOOM AND GUTS

Maiarch stopped grumbling when she reached the temple. She had grumbled she was hot and tired, that she had sore feet and stones in her sandals, she was thirsty and her knees ached.

'When you are a rich woman you can ride in a covered chair,' Antef promised. 'Four strong men will lift you…' He looked at the wobbling, wandering woman. 'Four *very* strong men will lift you. Maids will fan you and give you wine to cool you. Peasants will bow down as you pass in the street and say you are the greatest lady in Thebes.'

'I've got a stone in my other sandal now, Antef,' the old woman whined. 'Are we nearly there yet?'

'The temple is just outside the city gates and we're at the gates now,' he told her. He didn't tell her that the temple was a city itself and they had to walk through the shrines and the courtyards, past the grain stores and the animal pens to reach the Temple of Amun.

'Is it really worth it?' Maiarch asked in a sudden rage.

Antef kept calm. 'The whole of the Valley of the Kings is guarded. The only people who can get in are the priests and craftsmen working on new tombs. Do you want to be a rock cutter?'

'No,' she mumbled.

'So you have to be a priestess. The guards will get to

know you. They won't suspect you.'

Maiarch sighed, walked on and grumbled. She stopped grumbling when she reached the temple area. 'It's years since my old legs carried me outside the city,' she said softly. 'I'd forgotten.'

She wandered in wonder through the paths of the temples. Past the fountains and the gardens with the sweet blossoms. Past the animal pens with their stink. Past the smaller temples with the burning perfumes and past the larger temples with the smell of roasting sacrifices. Maiarch liked roasted meat.

Between you and me she liked anything you could put in your mouth and swallow. But greedy people don't like to be told they are greedy. Don't do it. Let's say aloud, 'Maiarch liked roast meat,' then mutter softly, 'and anything else she could wrap her grinning gums around.'

'It's … it's … it's a stone forest!' she sighed gaping up at the pillars that held the high roofs, some higher than the height of six men.

Inside, the walls were painted and even in the gloom the colours shone like a rainbow.

When they finally reached the Temple of Amun in the middle of all the smaller temples Maiarch had forgotten her grumbles. A tall priest stood in the entrance with a scroll. Antef pushed back his shoulders and marched up to him.

'Good morning, sir,' Antef said brightly. 'I've brought my sister Maiarch for the priestess training.'

The priest had a shaved head and sunken eyes. It looked as if a skull had been perched on the shimmering, white robe. A skull with an eagle-beak for a nose. He sniffed at Antef's sweaty smell and looked at a piece of papyrus in his hand. 'Maiarch?' he muttered. Then he barked, 'Maiarch? Don't have a Maiarch on my list. There's an Iti.' He glared at Maiarch. 'You're not an Iti by any chance, are you?'

'No, sir. I'm Maiarch,' the old woman whined.

'I know you're Maiarch. Your brother *said* you're Maiarch. But you're not on my list, are you? If you're not on my list you can't come in. We don't take any old beggar off the streets to be a priestess you know. Oh no. We are very fussy. *Very* fussy indeed.'

'How much?' Antef sighed.

'How much?'

'How much money do you want to add Maiarch to your list?' Antef asked.

The priest stretched himself like a vulture on a dead tree. His face turned red with rage. 'Are you trying to *bribe* me? Chief Priest of the Temple of Amun? Are you trying to *buy* your way into the holiest temple in Egypt? Do I *look* like the sort of man who can be bought and sold like a sack of corn? Do I?'

'Yes. How much?'

'I am insulted.'

'Ten obols?'

'Make it twenty,' the priest said quickly. 'I am top man here. Your sister will have the best training under my personal care.'

'Twenty.' Antef nodded and felt inside the purse that was hidden inside his tunic. 'Twenty buys her a place inside the tomb of Tutankhamun when he goes to the Valley of the Kings.'

The priest's dark eyes glittered. 'For thirty obols she can stay there after we seal the tomb. Travel with our falcon king all the way to the afterlife. What an honour!'

'Twenty,' Antef said.

The vulture swooped and the coins vanished under the shining white robe. 'It's a deal.' The priest turned to Maiarch: 'I seem to *have* your name on my list after *all*, my dear! Do come in and make yourself at home. Your first lesson this morning is praying and then a bit of sacrificing.'

He placed an arm around her shoulder and led her into the cool gloom of the temple. Maiarch looked back at Antef. He winked at her and waved before he turned and walked back to the city.

Maiarch smiled her toothless smile. 'What time is dinner?' she asked.

'Ah! You have to sacrifice first and *then* we have

dinner. The priests eat the sacrifice,' he explained.

'They do?' she gasped as he led her through the towering columns towards a stone altar at the darkest end of the temple. 'I always thought the sacrifices were a gift to the god Amun!'

The priest smiled a skull-like smile. 'We kill the animal then we roast it by the altar. Our lord Amun enjoys the smoke.'

'He eats smoke? Ooooh! I couldn't live on smoke,' Maiarch said.

'Amun can,' the priest said. 'Of course that leaves a lot of freshly roasted meat to be thrown away every day...'

'Or eaten,' Maiarch said happily.

'Or eaten.' The priest nodded.

Maiarch's snake tongue ran over her blubbery lips. 'I think I'm going to like it here.'

She sat on a bench by the altar while the priest looked along the line of new priest students. 'Good morning, everyone!'

'Good mor-ning High Priest,' the group chanted back.

'This morning we start with praying,' he said. 'We need lots of practice before the funeral of our falcon king. You will be taught prayers every morning. At the end of the week we will have tests.' Suddenly he lunged forward and his neck was almost as long as a vulture's. 'You, boy!'

'Me, sir? Yes, sir?' a weedy youth said.

'What will happen if you forget your prayers and fail the test?' the priest snapped.

'Please, sir, we get sacrificed to Amun?' he said.

The priest turned down his sour mouth in disgust. 'Stupid boy. Priests are far too valuable to sacrifice.' He swung round and pointed at a young woman. 'What do *you* think?'

'Please, sir, we get a bad report and we are expelled from the temple.'

'Correct. I can see you are going to make a fine priestess and the Temple of Amun will rise up to become top temple in the eyes of the King. If you fail you are not just letting yourself down, you are letting down Team Amun. And we wouldn't want that, would we?'

'No, High Priest,' the group said.

'So the first prayer we are going to learn today is the chant for King Ay. I say, "Tutankhamun is dead" and you reply, "Long live King Ay". I say, "The falcon is flown to heaven" and you reply, "King Ay is arisen in his place". Right, class shall we try it?'

The voices floated high above the altar and echoed past the pillars. It was a peaceful scene.

***

And it was peaceful in the city that afternoon as Antef led little Paneb to the School for Scribes.

'I have been to a school in Karnak. I know how to read and write,' Paneb complained.

Antef stopped. 'I thought Maiarch was bad enough, complaining all the way to the temple. You are worse, Twig-boy.'

'You told Dalifa not to call me that,' Paneb argued.

'And maybe I can see why Dalifa hates you so much. I will tell you one last time. I do not want a boy who can paint the signs inside the tomb. I want a head boy. I want the most important boy in the school inside the tomb when Tutankhamun is buried. I want you to be the most trusted. Understand? Now, do you have the scroll?'

'I worked on it all night,' Paneb said.

'And you wrote exactly what I told you?' Antef asked. Paneb nodded. 'Exactly.'

'Good. Then look over the wall here.'

The two thieves had reached a house with a courtyard. It was surrounded by a low wall. Boys sat on the ground with pots and brushes while an older boy walked around and swished at them with a stick to keep them working. Antef waved a hand and the head boy, the one with the stick, looked across at him. 'What do you want, scruffy old man? What business do you have in the School for Scribes?'

The head boy raised his eyebrows. 'With me? What business can you have with me, you slime from a crocodile's nose?'

'Wonderful news, young sir. Your fame has spread through Egypt,' Antef crooned like a dove.

'It has?' the head boy said with a faint smile. 'I am not surprised.'

'That is why King Ay wants you to go north to Alexandria. There are ancient pyramids there with painted walls,' Antef explained. 'They have been damaged by a storm. King Ay wants the finest scribes in the land to repair them. He chose you to go from Thebes.'

'Me?'

Antef placed a scroll in his hands. It had a wax seal with a sign that could have been the royal crown.

It COULD have been ... but it wasn't. Of course the scroll was a forgery. I have to explain this in case you are stupid – like the head boy – and believe the ridiculous story Antef told. Repeat after me, 'King Ay did NOT send this message.' Good. Then we can carry on. Just remember we are dealing with crooked minds here. Next time YOU get a message from a king just stop and say, 'Oh, yeah?'

The head boy unrolled it and read. 'King Ay commands his humble servant to make his way to the Pyramid of Cheops in the north. There he will join the royal paint squad. The head boy's place in the school will be taken by the talented little Paneb – he may look young but he is very good … only not so good as you, of course! Best of luck, have a good journey and don't forget to write. Oh, and by the way, set off at once. It will take you at least two months to get there so don't hang around. Off you go! Signed, King Ay. Oh, and by the way again, this is a secret message. Eat the scroll as soon as you have read it.'

The head boy ran to pack some food and money in a blanket while trying to stuff the dry papyrus into his mouth and chew it. Antef said, 'Paneb here will eat some for you if it will help?'

The head boy looked horrified. 'This is an order from my King,' he spluttered through the dried reeds. 'I must obey.'

'And you must away!' Antef added, pushing him through the gate and towards the road that led to the northern gate.

As the head boy chewed and choked and trotted, Antef patted Paneb on the shoulder. 'Three of you in place and still sixty-eight days to go. We will do it, Twig-boy. You and me, Maiarch, Neria and Dalifa … the Fabulous Five of Thebes really will pull off the greatest robbery in history!'

Pots, pouts and porridge

'And about time, too,' Dalifa snapped when Antef arrived at her house to take her to the jeweller's workshop. 'I am an important part of the Fabulous Five … you could say I am the MOST important part. Yet I am the *last* to be given a job.'

Antef spread his hands and began to explain. 'It was important…'

'Even Twig-boy got his job before me!'

'… that the tasks needing the most preparation…'

'And if you ask me, that Neria is too stupid to be part of the Fabulous Five.'

'… were given their posts first.'

'And Maiarch is probably too slow. I am as fast as an antelope and my wits are sharper than a crocodile tooth.'

Antef gave up. He let her run down like a water-clock.

She went on, 'I even worry about you – the so-called world's, so-called greatest, so-called thief! Hah! And you leave me till last. Are you sure you know what you're doing?'

Antef said the best thing. Nothing.

'Well?' the girl demanded. 'What are we waiting for?'

'I was waiting for you. I am taking you to the jeweller to work on Tutankhamun's ornaments.'

'I can't go like this,' Dalifa cried.

'Like what?'

'I haven't combed my hair or painted my eyes. My hair looks like a Nile reed bed after a storm.'

'I will wait, 'Antef said quietly. 'But you must be ready before the rising sun strikes the peak of Qurn.'

The girl looked at the lightening sky and ran inside to make herself ready. 'If you'd known you wanted me this early you should have called earlier,' she raged. Dalifa had a lot of rage inside her. Antef worried about that.

As the first rays of the sun crept over the desert, Dalifa ran out, ribbons trailing and eyes made huge with eye-paint. 'Come on!' she urged as she stomped down the street.

Antef picked up his cloth parcel and made his old legs trot after her. His knees were aching by the time they reached the end of the row of houses.

When he caught her he hissed, 'Just for once, Dalifa, let me do the talking. You are my stepdaughter…'

'No I'm not!'

'That is the story we agreed,' he moaned. 'We can't change it now.'

'Can't I be a princess from a distant land, looking to make my fortune in Egypt so I can meet a prince and join the royal family of Egypt?'

'No, Dalifa. You are my stepdaughter ... adopted.'

The girl made the pouting 'pah' noise with her lips and strode on. Antef clutched his bundle to his chest. His precious bundle. His stolen bundle.

The jeweller's workshop was a low building near the centre of the city. Some of the finest bracelets and necklaces, rings and hair jewels were spread on a stone table at the front. Two huge Nubian slaves stood guard and looked fiercely at Antef.

He smiled his gap-toothed smile at them. 'Hello, boys. Just here to see your master, Kheperu!'

One nodded silently for Antef and Dalifa to enter the house. The jeweller was a hairy little man. So hairy he had trouble keeping his beard plucked and his head shaved. Hairs bristled from his ears and nose and Dalifa turned up her sharp nose in disgust. He wore a thick belt and three brass keys hung from it on a brass hook.

'Kheperu!' Antef cried and hugged the little jeweller.

'What?' the jeweller asked suspiciously. 'Do I know you?'

'We met at the Festival of Opet!'

'I don't remember,' the hairy man frowned and his hairy eyebrows met in the middle. Well they would. They met in the middle even when he wasn't frowning.

'I thought you might not remember! You had a lot of strong beer to drink that night ... and of course you had that young dancing girl on your knee!'

'Sssshhhh!' Kheperu hissed and shook so much his keys jangled. 'My wife will hear!'

Antef smiled and whispered: 'She was a very pretty girl.'

'What can I do for you?' Kheperu said quickly.

Handshakes hadn't been invented. You may think it is pretty horrible to be hugged by a smelly man like Antef. YOU may imagine shaking hands is BETTER. But just think ... the person you meet may not have washed their hands before they shake yours! Where has that hand been? Yeuch! It's enough to make you give up shaking hands altogether and start rubbing noses like Eskimos. No. Snot a very good idea either.

'I hear you need extra workers to make the jewels for Tutankhamun's grave? I brought my stepdaughter Dalifa here to help you,' Antef explained.

Kheperu's mouth turned down, sour as if he'd drunk rotten wine. 'My workers train with me for five years before I allow them to create royal jewels. We cannot wait five years for this girl to be trained,' he snorted.

'I am a princess from a faraway land and I made wonderful jewels in my palace. I am here to meet a prince of Egypt!' Dalifa said grandly.

Kheperu leaned forward and spoke quietly in Antef's ear. 'Does the girl have a soft brain from too much time in the sun?'

'She's as sharp as a crocodile's tooth. And very pretty! As pretty as your dancing girlfriend!'

'Sssshhhh!' Kheperu hissed. 'Look, old man, I cannot give a girl a job just because she's pretty!'

Antef nodded wisely. 'Of course you can't. You will give her a job because she is the best stone-carver in Thebes!'

'Is she?'

Antef carefully unwrapped his cloth bundle and showed Kheperu a beautiful statue of a girl. It was studded with blue lazuli stones for eyes and wore a fine robe covered in beaten gold. The amber-painted skin looked as natural as Dalifa's own.

Kheperu took the statue to the door to look at it in the morning light. 'I made a statue like this for Tutankhamun's vizier when he died. This has been stolen from the grave!'

Antef's mouth gaped like a catfish. 'Ah ... yes ... no ... Dalifa here MADE the statue but she copied it from one she found in the market,' Antef lied.

'It has my mark on the bottom,' Kheperu said.

'Yes ... ah ... of course ... Dalifa copied everything ... including the mark!'

'She copied a stolen statue?'

'Yes.'

'So where is my statue? Why isn't it in the vizier's grave?'

'I put it back,' Antef said and his voice was getting higher as he grew desperate.

'Put it back?'

'As soon as I realized it had been stolen by one of those dreadful grave-thieves.'

'Like Antef?' Kheperu asked.

'Yes ... like awful Antef,' Antef agreed.
'And your name is...?'
'Erm...' Antef struggled to find a name.
'Bahari!' Dalifa put in. 'Stepdaddy Bahari.'
'Bahari's a village. Are you from there?'
'Does it matter?' Antef moaned. 'The point is the girl is a great stone-carver. And pretty as your dancing girlfriend.'
'I'll give her a job,' Kheperu said quickly.
Antef breathed a great sigh. 'Dalifa ... kind Kheperu here will look after you.'
'Thank you, Stepdaddy Bahari.'
'Who?'
'You!'
'Oh, yes!' Antef chuckled weakly. He turned to leave.
'Oh, Bahari!' Kheperu called.
'Who?'
'You!'
'Oh, yes.'
'I don't remember a dancing girl!' Kheperu whispered.
'You were *very* drunk,' Antef told him. 'But don't worry, your secret is safe with Antef.'
'Who?'
'Bahari!' Dalifa said loudly.
Antef scuttled away. Kheperu scowled and looked at Dalifa as if she were a dung beetle. 'Well, girl, we'd better set you to work.' He unhooked his keys and led the way into the workshop.
Dalifa followed happily. The square house had a corridor down the middle. On the left were two small workshops – one for Kheperu and one for Dalifa. On the

other side was one large workshop where stone-carvers were working on a large stone slab. Every room had a heavy door with a lock.

'What did your stepfather say your name was?' the jeweller asked.

'It's Dalifa ... but you can call me princess,' she grinned.

***

Antef wandered wearily down the street to the river. 'Maybe Dalifa's right. Maybe I am getting too old,' he muttered to himself. 'I tried to sell a statue to the man who made it! That's the sort of mistake that will get us all crucified. This will be my last robbery. The big one. I'll never need to take these risks again. I'll retire,' he decided. He felt better.

The early sun was already warm on his back as he reached the edge of the Nile. Fishermen were already launching their boats into the river and scattering angry ducks that clattered into the air. Antef caught a fisherman just as he was about to set off from the shore. 'Take me across the river, good sir,' he said.

'Why should I?' the man asked.

'Because the gods will see you doing a kindness for a poor old man. Your heart will weigh less,' Antef said. He grabbed the fisherman's arm in his claw of a hand. 'Ammit is waiting for you. She has the head of a crocodile, the front body of a lion and the backside of a hippo,' he went on, remembering Dalifa's savage tale. 'If your heart is too heavy with cruel deeds Ammit will use her crocodile mouth to chew it up and swallow it. For all time, you will have to die and die again and again and…'

'I'll take you,' the fisherman muttered and Antef climbed into the little boat with a secret smile. 'But sit very still,' the fisherman warned. 'Upset the boat and it won't be Ammit the crocodile that gets you … it will be a Nile crocodile.'

Antef showed his broken teeth. 'My heart is light. I am ready to meet Ammit,' he said happily.

'I've seen men after they've been eaten by a crocodile,' the fisherman said as he paddled. 'They will be meeting Ammit in fifty bits. So sit still.'

Antef sat still.

On the west bank the old man stepped out and thanked the fisherman. Then he set off on the road towards the Valley of the Kings. The same road Tutankhamun would be taking in nine weeks' time.

The difference is Antef would be walking and Tutankhamun would be carried. This is normal. Firstly, kings were carried everywhere. Secondly, Tut would have trouble walking, wrapped up in all those bandages. And I'm sure there is a third reason why Tut would not be walking. I just can't think of it at the moment.

The temples on the west bank were as fine as the ones in Thebes on the east bank. Pharaohs liked temples. As long as people were praying and sacrificing they would live on after death. Antef patted the statue and hurried on.

He walked past the Tombs of the Nobles where he'd stolen the statue. 'Good morning, dead nobles and priests!' he cried cheerfully. 'Hope you are comfortable in the afterlife? It must be a bit crowded with all of you in there! And so *boring*! Imagine being stuck forever with a bunch of priests. Hah! Excuse me if I don't join you just yet.'

He tramped through the village of Deir el-Medina where the tomb workers lived, and begged some breakfast from a kind-faced worker's wife. She gave him some thin porridge she was sharing with her children and showed him to their toilet pit. Then he was on his way again.

Antef followed the stream of workers round the foot of Mount Qurn and entered the Valley of the Kings.

He could see where the workers were busiest. 'That must be the tomb of Tut.' He nodded to himself. He followed a young worker up the path to where workers were sweating to remove the stone from the tomb.

'Who's the gang-leader this morning?' Antef asked the worker.

The young man waved a hand towards a skinny old worker who was wandering around giving orders. 'Nepher over there.'

Antef shook the desert dust off his tunic and walked over to the gang-leader. 'I've heard of you,' he said slyly. 'You must be the famous Nepher ... greatest of the gang-leaders.'

The leader turned his smiling eyes towards Antef and gave him an answer he didn't expect. 'And I've heard of you. You must be the famous Antef ... Lord of the Thieves!'

Antef almost dropped the precious statue in shock.

LOOK OUT!
MAKE WAY!
SORRY!
WATCH OUT MATE!
HEY!
BEHIND YOU!
PARDON ME
COMING THROUGH
DON'T MIND ME
WATCH YA' BACK!
OUCH!
MIND OUT!
OI!
SCUSE!
EXCUSE ME!
PARDON!

Horus, horrors and hatred

Old Nepher laughed and wrapped a friendly arm around Antef's shoulders. 'Come and sit in the shade away from the eye of Horus.'

He led the old thief into the shadow of a cliff and they sat down to share a leather sack of beer.

Nepher looked up at the sun. 'The eye of Horus is watching you, Antef. Doesn't that worry you? No matter where you walk he can see you.'

Antef shrugged. 'If I don't bother the gods then the gods won't bother me. That's the way I see it.'

'You steal from tombs. If the gods take their revenge it will be fearsome,' Nepher said. He squinted up at the sun.

'Look at Horus there, watching us with his one eye. Look what happened to him! He once had two eyes, the same as you and me.'

'So they say,' Antef mumbled and squirmed when he remembered the horror of Horus's tale.

'His Uncle Seth ripped out the eye of Horus and tore it to shreds. Aren't you worried the gods might do that to you?'

'It's an old story. It may not be true.'

Nepher shrugged. 'It must be true. Horus found the left eye and popped it back in. You can see the good eye up there in the sky – the eye we call the Sun. He let his eyes float over the earth to light it. The Sun is the strong right eye ... the Moon is his weak left eye. And they're watching you, Antef, night and day.'

Antef was uneasy. 'I'm more worried about the eyes of General Menes,' he sighed.

'And so you should be,' Nepher smiled. 'He was here only yesterday.'

'Here!' the thief cried and jumped as if he'd sat on a scorpion. 'What did he want?'

'He wanted to warn us that a Prince of Thieves called Antef was sure to come around some day soon. He told the gang-leaders what you look like. That's why I've been expecting you, Antef.'

'And?'

'And ... I have to listen to your plot and agree to go along with it,' the gang-leader said.

'Agree?'

'Yes. I have to tell you that, whatever you plan, I will help you. Then I am to report you to General Menes. He wants you to rob the grave. He wants to catch you in the act – that way he can punish you and save the King's treasure.'

Antef's mouth was dry with fear and he took a long swig of the warm beer. 'Why are you telling me this?' he asked the gang-leader.

Nepher looked into Antef's eyes and said, 'Menes says I will get my reward in heaven. But I reckon a thief like you will give me a reward in this life! I'd rather have the reward now, Antef. What is your plan? And how much are you planning to pay me?'

Antef took a deep breath. 'Why should I trust you?'

'Because you have no choice. You have come here to get my help. Without it the whole plot will fail. Anyway you are a peasant. I am a peasant. We need to work together – together against the lords and the kings, their soldiers and their priests. Ordinary men and women against the rulers who hate us and need us. It's always been that way. It always will be.'

Antef nodded. He had decided. He liked the man. He trusted him.

There are some people who say, 'Trust nobody. Not never, not no way, not no how.' Apart from being very bad use of the English language, it is also a very bad way to live your life. Trust me, I know. But was Antef right to trust Nepher? Hah! You'll have to read on to find out. Maybe he was right – maybe he wasn't. I don't know. I'm just the writer.

'I will pay you with this statue,' he said and unwrapped the bundle. He passed the statue to Nepher.

The gang-leader handled it carefully. He turned it slowly and looked at the pictures that decorated it. 'Stolen?'

'Of course.'

'I could be called a thief if I try to sell it.'

'So don't sell it.' Antef shrugged. 'Keep it. One day, when you are too old to work, you can sell it. Keep the statue now and it will keep you in your old age.'

Nepher nodded. 'I accept. Now what is the plan?'

Antef narrowed his eyes. 'I cannot tell you all of the plan. I am putting my life in your hands … but there are others in the plot with me. I can't put their lives in your hands too.'

'I understand. So what do you want me to do?'

'You are the oldest of the gang-leaders?'

'I am the oldest.'

'So you will be given the job of filling in the tunnel to the tomb after the King is buried?'

'I will.'

'Then I want your gang to fill it in a special way…'

'Which way?'

And Antef told him…

What do you mean? You want me to tell you how Antef wanted the tunnel filled? Well I'm not going to. Just wait till the end of the book like everybody else. Anyway, if you had half a brain you'd work it out for yourself. Remember this is a TRUE story – some ancient peasant grave-robber thought of the plot. Why can't you? You with your computers and your internet and your beef-burger bloated brain?

***

After ten days there was a feast day in the city and all the workers were given a holiday. The Fabulous Five Thieves met in Antef's house again. Together for the first time since the day Tutankhamun died.

Five happy people. Five people working to a plan that was going well. Of course they had their grumbles.

Big Neria found work in the stinking House of Death a bit gruesome. Wouldn't you?

'Remember the morning you left me with the Priest of Anubis? He said my first job was scooping the brains out of an old priest – they said he wasn't very important and I could practise on him.'

'Easy enough job – even for you,' Dalifa snorted.

Big Neria looked upset. 'Easy? Have you ever tried taking someone's brain out?'

'It's funny you should say that, Neria, but I have never tried taking someone's brain out! If you say it's fun I will practise on Twig-boy here ... if I can find his brain,' she sneered.

Antef sighed. 'Dalifa, control your sharp tongue or you'll cut yourself.'

She made a 'puh' sound and sniffed.

Antef turned to Neria. 'I'm sure you need a lot of skill to work in the House of Death,' he said to soothe the big man.

'I do! I had to stick a copper wire up the old priest's nose and swirl it round till his brain was as mushy as porridge, then scoop bits out with a spoon.'

'Easy enough.' Dalifa shrugged.

'Nah! They ran all the way up my arm and dribbled on to the floor,' Neria cried. 'The priests made me scoop them up from the sand. Then I had to stand next to the Priest of Anubis with a pen made from a reed and a pot of ink.'

'Important job,' Dalifa sniffed. 'Pen holder. Were you strong enough to carry the pen *and* the ink?'

Neria glared at her. He turned to the others and explained. 'The Priest of Anubis marked a line about the length of his hand on the old man's side. Then in came a man in a black hood and a black robe. Scary!'

'A bandit?'

'That's what I thought. But he was a special sort of mummy man. He took a sharp stone knife from his belt and sliced along the line the Priest of Anubis had just drawn. He stuffed his hand into the body, wriggled it around and ripped out the stomach. Another priest took it and wrapped it in a cloth. They gave it to me!'

'Nice,' Maiarch chuckled.

'I was told to take it to a stone jar and stuff it in.'

'They're called canopic jars,' Paneb said quietly.

'Ooooh! They're called canopic jars,' Dalifa mimicked. 'Who's a clever little Twig-boy then?'

Neria went on, 'They did the same with the liver, kidneys, lungs and guts. Then a weird thing happened...'

'Did the guts jump back out of the jars?' Dalifa asked. 'Did they wrap themselves around your neck and strangle you? They do say there is a curse on those who steal from a mummy!'

'Shut up, Dalifa,' Antef said wearily. 'Carry on, Neria.'

'Well, the priests began to jeer at the man in the black hood and call him names like: "Desert dog!" "Filthy rat!" "Snake with the smell of Hippo's bum!" "Corpse-fly!" and "Snot-drip from the tip of an old man's nose!"'

'That's weird,' Maiarch agreed. 'But why did they do it to the poor man?'

'The ripper's job is an unclean job. He does his duty then the priests have to drive him out of the House of Death because he's an unclean man. It's a game really. But he's an important man. One day I may get to be the ripper!'

Antef sighed. 'No you won't, Neria. You are only there for sixty more days then we do the robbery and you'll never have to work again.'

'I forgot,' Neria sighed. 'It's just so interesting. If I wasn't a robber I'd want to be an embalmer!

Somebody had to do it I suppose – and they must have enjoyed it ... a bit like undertakers today ... or other really disgusting jobs that you think no one would EVER want to do. It would be bad enough if your dad was an undertaker – all the jokes about you living in the dead centre of your town – but what if he was something worse? What if he was ... a traffic warden? Or a grave-digger? Or a history teacher?

'Next week they're going to let me wash the corpses with palm wine – inside and out.'

Little Paneb felt a bit sick. 'But did you see the body of

Tutankhamun?' he asked.

'Oh, yes. The chief embalmers were working on him, of course. They'd put his liver and lungs, his stomach and intestines in the jars and filled his body with salt to dry it out. In a few weeks they'll start wrapping the body.'

'Ahhhh!' fat Maiarch breathed. 'Will they wrap precious jewels in the bandages?'

'Lots of jewels ... and magic writing,' Neria said. 'But I never had the chance to steal any jewels.'

'No! No! That will come later,' Antef muttered. 'The main thing is, you got the job of carrying the coffin to the funeral?'

'I did, and they gave me a belt for my tunic with the royal seal on it. That allows me to go anywhere in the tombs or the palaces.'

'Then that's the first part of the plot!' Antef grinned. 'So how did you get on in the temple, Maiarch?' Antef asked.

Dalifa sprang to her feet. 'Why her? Why can't I report on how I got on at the jeweller's? It's not fair. I'm going to tell you anyway!' she shouted.

She stood in the centre of the room and half closed her eyes. She pictured the story she was telling. 'I work in the stone room carving the statues out of alabaster. It's dusty, thirsty work ... but I am very good!'

'That's why we chose you, Dalifa,' Maiarch chuckled.

'The room is locked every night because some of my statues have precious stones set into them. Now, next door Kheperu works on the gold and jewellery. No one is allowed into that room even when he is working. The walls are double-thick stone and the Nubians take turns to guard the outside day and night so no one can break in.'

YUCK!
YUM!

'But what about Tutankhamun's door?' Paneb asked.

'I'm coming to that, Twig-boy ... there is a third room across the corridor – the largest room – and all there is in there is a large slab of stone. The stone that will be the door to Tutankhamun's tomb. Every day carvers work on it, engraving pictures and signs. I tried telling Kheperu that I could do stone-carving like that but he wouldn't let me.'

'And is the door to their workroom locked?' Maiarch asked.

Dalifa nodded. 'Every night after work Kheperu goes round and locks all three rooms. No one can get in ... not even Paneb the housebreaker.'

'We could if we had those keys,' Paneb said.

'They never leave Kheperu's belt,' Dalifa said. 'I'm sure he sleeps with them round his scrawny neck.'

'It's a problem but we have some weeks left to find a way round it,' Antef said. 'The main thing is you are in the workshop house and Kheperu trusts you. We'll find a way around the key problem, don't worry. Now, sit down, Dalifa,' Antef ordered. 'Show Maiarch some respect for her age. It was her turn to report on her work, not yours.'

'Puh!' Dalifa sat and flumped back on to the bench. 'I don't care how old she is, she's not as important as I am. You should all remember that. If I walk away then you are all in real trouble. Real trouble,' she threatened.

'When thieves fall out then their crimes will be discovered,' said a voice from the doorway.

'General Menes!' Paneb squeaked.

The large man stepped into the gloom and his face of bronze had a crease that might have been a smile. 'So glad to see you haven't forgotten me!'

Temples, terror and Tutankhamun

'How are the plans going, Antef?' the King's guard asked.

'Plans? What plans?' Antef asked.

'We do have a plan,' Maiarch said happily. 'A plan to celebrate the crowning of the new King Ay with a brew of strong beer! Is it against the law, General Menes?'

Menes gave her a look as cold as a crocodile's heart. 'I too have plans.'

'To brew beer?' Dalifa asked cheekily.

'Plans to find out what you are up to,' the General said.

Antef knew about those plans. Antef knew that the gang-leader Nepher was the General's spy. But Antef didn't want to tell his team of thieves. They would worry if they knew the risk Antef was taking.

Antef just nodded. 'That's why I'd never dream of trying to rob a tomb,' he admitted. 'I could never outwit you, General.'

Menes gave him one of his cold stares and said, 'Maiarch here is working at the Temple of Amun. The skinny boy has cheated his way into a scribe school. The girl with the painted face is in the royal jeweller's workshop. I don't know where stupid Neria is working but I have weeks to find out.'

Maiarch spread her hands. 'We are honest citizens of Thebes,' she cried. 'We are all doing honest work.'

'So what is Antef doing?' Menes asked softly.

'Wrestling crocodiles,' he said.

Even Menes' hard face showed shock. 'What?'

'Thebes will be full of people from all over Egypt,' the old man explained. 'They will come here for the funeral. They will drink and eat ... but they will want to be entertained. I used to work for a magician, you know. I am too old for that now. So, I plan to set up a show ... I will wrestle with crocodiles. The greatest show in Egypt. It will make me my fortune ... if the crocodiles don't eat me first.'

Menes grabbed the front of Antef's tunic. 'My bite is worse than any crocodile. The crocodile will kill you quickly. I promise to kill you slowly ... when I catch you,' he spat before he turned and stalked out of the door.

Antef had shown no fear on his wrinkled face but there was sweat running down his whip-scarred back as the General left.

Neria turned to him. 'Great idea ... wrestling crocodiles. Will you let me watch?'

Dalifa groaned. 'Neria, you really are as stupid as you look. Antef was having a little *joke*. He couldn't wrestle a catfish.'

'Yes I could!' Antef cried. 'I would probably lose ... but fetch me a catfish and I'll show you.'

Even little Paneb joined in the laughter and the group relaxed again. 'Talking about wrestling with creatures, you should see the trouble I had in the temple with a goat,' Maiarch said. 'I was just going to tell you about it before the General arrived.'

'I like goats,' Paneb said quietly.

'Ooooh! He likes goats,' Dalifa snorted.

'I had to wear a lot of uncomfortable clothes and do some disgusting things,' Maiarch said.

'Not as disgusting as sticking a knife in a corpse and pulling his intestines out!' Neria grumbled.

'Every bit as bad!' Maiarch argued. 'I mean to say, I get my meat from a butcher in the market ... when I can afford it.'

The others nodded. Antef said, 'I usually eat bread and onions but I have tasted meat. When I am rich ... after the robbery ... I will eat meat every day.'

'But I'd never had to kill my own meat before!' Maiarch said and she shuddered.

'They made you kill something before you could eat it?' Dalifa asked.

'Every day they sacrifice a kid goat to the god Amun. One day the High Priest said it was my turn. They gave me a goat and told me to cut its throat, collect the blood in a bowl and cook the rest.'

'Did you do it?' Paneb gasped.

'I did *not*,' she said, a little ashamed. 'I took the goat to a butcher and swapped it for a bowl of blood and some cooked goat meat. The priests never knew.'

'Did Amun drink the blood?' Neria wanted to know.

'Amun is a stone statue, Neria. They make sacrifices to him and the peasants think Osiris drinks the blood, but he doesn't.'

'So, who eats the cooked meat?' Dalifa asked.

Maiarch spread her hands. 'The priests, of course!

They have it for their evening meal.'

'Poor Osiris must get hungry,' Neria grumbled.

'He ... is ... a ... stone ... oh, never mind! You are so stupid, Neria!' Dalifa wailed.

'But the plot,' Antef reminded Maiarch. 'Did you get a job in the funeral of King Tutankhamun?'

Maiarch nodded once. 'I travel with the funeral all the way. From the temple, over the river and all the way to the tomb.'

'Ahhhh!' Antef breathed. 'That is another piece of the plan in place.'

'Then I hope I never have to go back to that blood-soaked temple again,' Maiarch said. 'The Chief Priest of Amun is a terrifying man – and this morning he reminded us all of the hideous punishments we would suffer if there is a theft at the funeral. I think he was hinting we may end up like the goats.'

Even Big Neria looked worried. When the curtain at the door swung back he had to choke back a scream.

An ugly head peered into the gloom. 'Dalifa?' he said. The hair in his nose and ears sprouted like weeds in a cornfield.

'Kheperu?' Dalifa said. 'What do you want?'

As the little jeweller stepped into the room there were tiny movements he didn't notice. Antef signed to Paneb for the boy to get behind the visitor. The boy, silent as a shadow, moved slowly into place.

'We have an urgent order from the palace. They have decided they want some extra funeral statues,' the jeweller said.

'But it's a holiday!' she argued.

'We cannot refuse to serve the palace,' Khepuru said sternly.

Antef made another sign and Paneb moved closer to the jeweller. Dalifa saw what they were doing and decided to make a scene to take Kheperu's attention away from the boy.

'There is plenty of time,' Dalifa said, rising to her feet and stamping her foot in anger. 'The funeral is weeks away.'

Then as Paneb's hand stole towards the jeweller's belt she began to scream in his face. 'You're a slave-driver, Kheperu, a slave-driver! I work my fingers to the bone for you and still you want more! Cruel, cruel man!' she sobbed and beat his chest with her fists.

As he raised his hands to save himself Paneb stretched *his* hand forward and slipped the keys off the jeweller's belt. Then he tiptoed quickly to the door and slipped outside.

Kheperu sighed. 'Bahari … tell your daughter to obey.'

'Who?' Big Neria asked.

'Bahari,' Dalifa said quickly pointing to Antef. 'He's my stepfather.'

'I never knew that!' Neria smiled.

Antef jumped to his feet and took Dalifa firmly by the elbow. He dragged her towards the door and shooed Kheperu out.

Dalifa struggled but Antef was strong and she was soon standing in the dusty air from the road outside. 'Dalifa would *love* to work on her holiday … because she knows you will pay her double, Kheperu!'

'I will?' the hairy jeweller scowled.

'You will,' Antef nodded. 'And Dalifa will be able to buy herself those silk ribbons she has always wanted.'

Dalifa grinned. 'And what will you buy me … Step-daddy?'

'A golden ring for your finger … once Tutankhamun has been buried,' Antef promised. 'Now go with nice Kheperu and work.'

As Kheperu turned to walk back to his shop he didn't see Dalifa stick out her tongue at Antef before she turned to follow him.

Please note the writer of this book is not excusing such rude behaviour. I would never encourage anyone to stick out their tongue at their elders. It is not only rude it is dangerous. Your tongue could be pecked by a passing pigeon. A long tongue, like yours, could trail along the ground and trip up a passing nun. Do NOT do it.

Little Paneb appeared around the corner of the house from the toilet pit at the back. He held up the keys for Antef. 'Good boy. Did you press them into some mud so we can copy them later?'

'Yes,' Paneb said.

'The ground is dry,' Antef said frowning.

'Not after I piddled on it,' Paneb shrugged.

'Urgh!' the old man said and held the keys away from himself in disgust. He called down the dusty street, 'Kheperu!'

The jeweller turned. 'Yes?'

'My boy found these keys on the floor of the house. You haven't dropped any keys, have you?'

Kheperu's hand flew to his belt and he gasped. 'My keys! My precious keys!' He trotted back to where Antef stood and snatched them from the thief's hand. 'They're a bit damp, aren't they?' he asked.

'You dropped them in a beer cup,' Paneb said quickly.

The jeweller nodded, turned and walked away. 'He didn't say thank you,' Paneb said.

Antef laughed softly. 'We will have the keys copied. We will carry out the funeral plot. Then you can go to his workshop any time you like and rob him over and over again. Not many burglars have keys, do they, Paneb?'

The boy smiled shyly. 'And it will serve Kheperu right.'

Antef slapped his shoulder and went to collect the mud models of the keys from the back of the house.

As Antef turned he saw a tiny movement at the end of the street. Almost the shadow of a movement. It was as if a ghostly face had been peering round the corner, watching.

'There are no such things as ghosts,' Antef muttered. 'General Menes is having us watched.'

***

Antef went back inside the house and sat down. 'It is becoming dangerous,' he said. 'The General knows what we are all doing – except Neria … and he may find out about your mummy-making any day.' The old man looked hard at Neria. 'The General has spies on the streets. When you leave here you will be followed.'

'I'll smack him on the head with my club,' Neria promised.

'And that will give Menes an excuse to have you executed – attacking a palace guard, even a spying one, would be a serious mistake,' Antef explained. 'We haven't broken any laws yet. We won't break one … till we rob the tomb of King Tut.'

Maiarch stuffed a date into her mouth and chewed on it noisily, spitting bits of date out as she spoke. 'Does it matter if Menes knows where Neria works?' she asked.

'It *might* do. Once he knows what we are all doing now he may work out what we'll be doing on the day of the funeral,' Antef said slowly, trying to work out how the General would think.

'I've another idea!' Neria said brightly. 'Why doesn't one of you put on my headscarf and my tunic and walk out of the door? The spy will think it is me leaving and follow the wrong person!'

Antef looked at the big man and spoke gently. 'Neria, there is no one here half the size of you ... at least Maiarch is as wide as you but we are all half as tall.'

Neria nodded eagerly. 'So one person has to sit on the shoulders of another and let my tunic cover them both! Maiarch can sit on Paneb's shoulders.'

Antef thought about it. 'I think little Paneb may be squashed slightly smaller than a scarab beetle,' he said. 'But perhaps Paneb can sit on my shoulders. Let's try it!' A few beats of the water-clock later and a strange figure ducked through the doorway wearing Neria's headscarf and tunic and carrying Neria's club. It wobbled down the street towards the river.

The curtain over the door opened a little and Maiarch's watery eye looked out. The eye watched as a man slipped out from behind a wall and followed the road to the river. Maiarch smiled. 'Off you go, Neria. Back to the House of Death. Stay there in a worker's tent. We won't see you again till the night before the King's funeral.'

Neria lumbered out dressed only in his loincloth and

hurried off towards the desert. Maiarch smiled. Satisfied.

On the waterfront Paneb climbed down from Antef's shoulders; the two thieves mixed with the fishermen and became lost in the crowd. A spy cursed the name of Horus and wondered if General Menes would forgive him ... or if there'd be another funeral soon!

Days, doors and destruction

Days passed the way days usually do. The right eye of Horus floated across the sky and scorched the desert. Then the left eye came out and moonlight shone down on Thebes.

Thebes slept. You could hear it snoring.

Who said, 'Cities don't snore'? They do. As soon as you fall asleep the city falls asleep and the city snores. When you wake up the city stops snoring. That is why you will never hear it. You will just have to trust me when I say the city of Thebes was snoring that night.

Even the Nubian guards outside the house of Kheperu dozed. They sat on mats and rested against the stone wall – the outside wall to the treasure room. No one was going to chisel a way through that wall while they were there. And no one could get into the room from the inside because the massive doors in the corridor were locked. Kheperu slept with the keys.

But Dalifa didn't need to chisel through the wall. She didn't even want to get into the treasure room. She slipped into the front door of the workshop, and walked past her carving room. She turned away from Kheperu's treasure room and came to the door that the stone workers used.

Dalifa tried one of the keys that Antef had copied. It didn't work. She tried the second one and it slipped into the lock beautifully. The girl twisted it and the greased lock slipped open.

She pushed the door. It creaked on its leather hinges. She smelled the stale sweat-smell that the workmen had left behind. This room had a small window to let in light and air. It had bronze bars to keep out slippery thieves like Paneb ... not that anyone would want to steal what was in the room. It was just a carved stone door. A door that was almost ready for Tutankhamun's tomb.

Dalifa locked the room from the inside. It made the room dark. But she was going to make a noise and she needed to shut that noise inside the room.

Antef had wanted to come with her. 'You're too slow to run away if something goes wrong,' she told him.

'Let me send Neria to protect you,' Antef had begged.

'He's too big and clumsy. We agreed he has to stay at the House of Death until the funeral. Anyway, even Big Neria can't fight those two Nubian guards if they catch us.'

'Then take little Paneb to keep watch,' Antef had groaned.

Dalifa glared at him. 'This is my job. This is what we've spent weeks planning. I know what to do and I don't need any help.' Suddenly she had shouted, 'What's wrong? Don't you trust me?'

'Of course I do!' Antef said. 'You will do a wonderful job…'

'I *meant* trust me to keep quiet if they catch me. If they torture me do you think I'll betray you? Because I won't. If I get caught they can cut out my tongue and I still wouldn't talk!'

Paneb sniggered. 'If they cut out your tongue you'd never talk again!'

For a moment Antef thought Dalifa was going to hit the boy. But she breathed deeply and fought back her temper. 'Paneb,' she said quietly. 'I sometimes wonder if you know how dangerous this is. When it comes to *your* part of the plan will *you* be brave? And will *you* betray us if you're caught?'

Paneb had looked a little ashamed at that. 'Sorry, Dalifa,' he had mumbled.

Dalifa just nodded to show he was forgiven.

But now, in the stone-carvers room it was dark. The left eye of Horus was peering at her through the barred window. Now she was more afraid than she'd ever been in her life. Dalifa fumbled on the workbench and felt a bronze chisel. Her hand was shaking so much the chisel dropped from her hand and fell with a clatter on to the stone floor.

The clang rang round the room and she was sure the whole of Thebes must have heard it and woken up. She went still and felt sweat running down into her eyes. But there were no sounds of running guards. She breathed again.

Dalifa felt the floor and found the chisel. This time she

gripped it firmly. Then she took a wooden hammer from the workbench and moved to the back of the decorated door.

She measured from the top of the door down the side. 'One cubit,' she mumbled, the length of her fingertips to her elbow. She wrapped a scarf around the chisel and struck the door to make a mark at one cubit.

The wooden hammer made little noise when it hit the chisel. The chisel bit into the stone but the sound was muffled by the scarf.

Then she measured a cubit along the top of the door and made another mark. There was still no sound from outside so she began to chisel carefully. Dalifa cut a line across the stone. The line joined the cubit mark along the top to the cubit mark down the side.

She worked steadily but it was slow. She wished she'd brought water with her. The weak left eye of Horus was sliding down the sky and the strong right eye was nowhere to be seen. It was really dark in the workshop now but the carved line was so deep she could feel her way along it. Dalifa's tunic was sticking to her body with sweat. For once she was glad she had left off her eye-paint as it would have been running down her face.

At last Dalifa knew she was halfway through the stone. She paused. This was the dangerous part. She put down the small hammer and chisel and found the big hammer. It was made of wood but almost too heavy for her to lift. Maybe she should have brought Neria after all.

She raised it over her head and let it fall against the top corner of the door that she had weakened with her line. But she hadn't the strength to damage the door. She groaned. The sun was turning the sky grey now. Thebes would be stirring soon. Kheperu would be coming into the workshop and would catch her with the damaged door. Did she have to spend more precious time making her chiselled line deeper?

'Can I help?' came a whispered voice.

Dalifa choked back the scream that was rising in her throat. She looked up at the barred window. The small hands of Paneb clutched at the bars as he pulled himself up and looked in.

'Paneb?'

'Can I help?'

'How?'

'Two of us on the hammer.'

'I'll open the door and let you in. Mind the guards aren't on patrol,' she said quickly.

But Paneb just pulled on the bars, slipped his head through then his shoulders. His hips stuck for a while but moments later he was in and dropping to the floor beside Dalifa. 'That was amazing!' she said.

Paneb shrugged. 'It's what I do best.'

Suddenly Dalifa threw her arms around him. 'Oh, Twig-boy I never thought I'd be pleased to see you.' Her face was wet as tears mingled with the sweat. She hugged him.

Paneb wriggled free. 'Urgh! Don't do that! We need to work quickly.'

'I'm just trying to show you how grateful I am,' she said.

'Then do it later...' he began and swallowed. Hard. 'No! I didn't mean that ... I meant ... we're a team. You don't have to show me anything at all. Don't do anything later. Go away. Pick up the hammer...'

'Which do you want me to do? Go away or pick up the hammer?' she snapped.

Paneb reached for the hammer. They arranged their hands on the handle and rocked it gently. 'When I say "three" we hit the top corner,' Paneb said. 'One ... two ... three!'

The hammer hit the weakened corner with a soft thunk. The stone cracked and fell. It hit the floor with a crash loud enough to wake Tutankhamun.

Paneb and Dalifa looked at one another. 'You escape, Twig-boy,' Dalifa said. 'I'll take my chances here.'

Paneb nodded. He grabbed the bars, pulled himself out into the morning light and ran off before the guards circled the building. Moments later Dalifa heard them talking outside the window. She didn't understand their language but they seemed to be saying, 'Where did that bleeding crash come from? Inside? Or outside?'

'Nothing out here ... let's check inside.'

I could write this in ancient Nubian for you if you wish. If you are an ancient Nubian reader you will know the second guard said, 'Edisni kcehc s'tel ... ereh tuo gnihton'. But in future please do your own translations as I want to get on with the story and find out what happens.

Dalifa held her breath till it hurt and listened as their sandals shuffled away. She didn't hear them in the corridor outside the room because the door to the room was too thick. But she did hear them rattle at the handle and say, 'Locked!' They walked away.

She waited 50 heartbeats then carefully unlocked the door. The corridor was silent. She locked the door behind her then crept out of the front door. The guards were back at their post outside the treasure room.

She ran home, the morning air making her tunic stick to the cooling sweat on her back. By the time she had changed into her work-tunic, put on her eye-paint and curled and ribboned her hair it was time to leave for work.

Dalifa was exhausted through lack of sleep but satisfied with her night's work.

When she returned to Kheperu's workshop she heard him wailing. 'The door! The door to Tutankhamun's tomb! Ruined! It has to be delivered tomorrow. The door is ruined and I am ruined! I think I'll have to kill myself. Aieeee!'

Kheperu turned to the Nubian guards. 'Kill me! Before

King Ay finds out I've let him down. Kill me quickly!'

The Nubians looked at one another and one said, 'Rettun.'

Kheperu snatched the club from one guard and hit himself hard on his head. 'Ouch! I hurt myself! Ouch! There has to be a better way!'

'There is,' Dalifa said. She was standing at the open door. The stone masons, Kheperu and the guards looked at her.

'What?' Kheperu blinked.

'My real father, the Prince of Tyre, had a broken door just like that.'

'Poor man,' Kheperu sighed.

'He fixed it,' Dalifa said quietly.

'Fixed it?'

'The door.'

'How?'

'Let me show you.'

The girl told the masons to pick up the broken triangle of stone and put it back in place. 'Now,' she said, 'all you have to do is stick it back in place.'

'With what?' Kheperu asked crossly.

'Plaster,' Dalifa said. 'Send the guards to the scribe school. They use plaster to make smooth panels. They paint and write on the plaster. It's mixed with water, and it sets hard when it dries. Get it now and the repair will be dry before it goes to the tomb tomorrow!'

Kheperu looked at her in wonder. 'Oh, princess, you may have saved my life.' He turned to the guards. 'Fetch some plaster from Paneb, at the scribe school.' They hurried off to obey.

The guards asked Paneb for some 'retsalp' but that wasn't a problem ... he'd been expecting them. It was all part of the plan.

Dalifa mixed the plaster and used it to glue the broken piece back in place. Kheperu sighed. 'The plaster is cream, the stone is grey. The join shows.'

Dalifa smiled. 'I know.' She bent down and scooped up the stone dust and chippings that covered the floor. Before the plaster set she rubbed the stone dust into the plaster. It turned grey. 'See?' she said. 'In the gloom of the tomb no one will ever notice.'

Kheperu was almost crying with happiness. 'Dalifa, come to my workshop ... choose any jewel you want. You are the most wonderful girl in Thebes.'

'I'm not.'

'You're not?'

'I'm not the most wonderful girl in Thebes. I'm the most wonderful girl in the whole of Egypt.' She smiled.

Kheperu didn't argue.

ANTEF, ART AND ANTS

Weeks passed. First one week then another.

Strange how weeks usually do it in that order: 'One week then another'. If we had 'another then one week' we'd go back in time. And that is how I travelled back to ancient Egypt to bring you this story. That is how I (and now you) are the only people who still understand Ancient Nubian talk. Some day the whole world will speak Naibun Tneicna. But we haven't time to stop and teach them just yet. I need to tell you what happened after the weeks had passed.

The water-clock dripped on into the second hour of the afternoon – the afternoon before the funeral. 'They'll be preparing the funeral soon,' Antef told the team. 'The body will be put in its first coffin, so you'd better get across to the House of Death, Neria, and keep an eye on it.'

Neria had sneaked back into Thebes to check that the plan was still going ahead. The big man nodded and lumbered to his feet. 'I'll see you all at the tomb at sunrise,' he said with a nervous smile. He ducked his head under the door frame and went out into the white heat of the afternoon.

Maiarch rose and said, 'And the priests will be preparing everything too. I'd better get back to the temple before they miss me.' She looked at them with her sharp eyes.

'Till the tomb at sunrise, then,' she said and she was gone.

Antef stretched and looked at Paneb. 'You're not needed in the scribe's school?' he asked.

The boy shook his head. 'Everything is done. The best scribes in the school have been working in the tomb ever since it was finished. We plastered the walls and painted in the pictures and the prayers. The ones who stayed in the school wrote the Books of the Dead for the priests to wrap in Tutankhamun's bandages.'

'If you are not busy you can do a small painting for me, young Paneb,' Antef said. 'You can draw me a picture of the tomb and its rooms. You went inside with the painters – I only got as far as the door.'

Paneb nodded eagerly and picked up his paint-pots and brushes. He took an old piece of papyrus and quickly sketched a plan of the tomb and passed it to Antef.

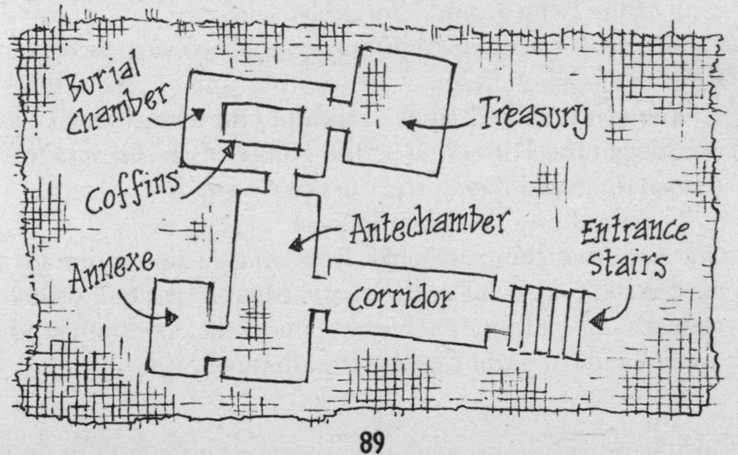

Dalifa looked over his shoulder and moved the palm-oil lamp to get a better view. None of them realized at first that it had gone dark in the room. There was a soft sound behind them and Antef swung round. He discovered then why the room had grown dim – the light from the doorway was blocked by the wide form of General Menes.

His bronze-hard face was scarred from battle blows and his voice was harsh as a vulture's cry. 'Antef – grave-robber. I want a word with you and your friends.'

'We've done nothing!' Antef said quickly.

'Tutankhamun's widow has sent me to check on the grave-robbers of Thebes. So what are you plotting?' the soldier asked.

Antef shrugged. 'The boy was just showing us how the walls of the tomb are painted,' he said.

'So show me,' the soldier said and he knelt beside him.

The soldier picked up the sketch. 'This looks like a plan of the King's tomb, Antef,' he said.

'Really!' The old man gasped. 'You surprise me, General.'

The soldier clutched at his knife and straightened. 'I am Menes and I am not a simple soldier. I am General of the palace guard. Don't treat me like a fool.'

'Sorry, officer,' Antef smiled.

'I saw that lumpen Neria leave here a few moments ago. What part is he in the plot?' Menes asked. 'Coffin-carrier?'

Antef tried to answer but his mouth was too dry to speak. Dry with fear because General Menes had already guessed a small part of the plot. He went on, 'And I suppose the boy is a scribe who went in to the tomb to spy out the plan. The priestess Maiarch will be a great help – I saw her leave. And the girl here has been working on decorating the coffin, I expect.'

'No!' Antef said. He was telling the truth for once. Menes didn't have the full picture.

'She's been making…' Paneb began.

'Shut up, boy!' Antef said savagely. 'The good officer doesn't want to know about that!'

'Oh, but I do,' General Menes said.

Antef said, 'Dalifa has always made ornaments and little statues. So, of course, she was happy to offer her skills to make ornaments for dead Tutankhamun's tomb.'

General Menes nodded. 'She will have made the ornaments so you know what is going in. And then you will help Antef to take them out again. Melt the gold and silver down and make new ones to sell and make your fortune!'

'No!' Antef laughed. 'We would never rob the grave of our dear, dead King. Never!'

'Good,' General Menes grinned. 'Because if you try it, and if I catch you, I will tie you to a tree. Then I will cut off your ears and then your nose. Then I will cut off little strips of skin one at a time and pour salt water into the cuts. Then I will let the ants and the jackals finish you off. Would you like that, Antef?'

The old man shook his head.

The General rose and left.

'We can't go ahead now,' Paneb said.

Antef looked at the empty doorway. 'Oh, yes we can, Paneb. I have spent all my money on this plot. There is no turning back now. He is clever. But he hasn't guessed about Dalifa's damaged door. So long as he doesn't know about that he will never work out how we plan to do the robbery. The greatest robbery in history.'

In the warm room little Paneb shivered. 'Antef,' he snivelled, 'I don't want to have my ears cut off! I'd scream!'

Antef threw his head back and laughed. 'If your ears were cut off you wouldn't hear yourself!'

'It's not funny,' the boy cried.

The old man reached across, grabbed his tunic and hissed, 'General Menes was just guessing. He knows nothing. Anyway, he is just one man. He can't stop us.'

Dalifa said, 'Twig-boy's frightened.'

'Listen, you two, I know what I am doing. We are not going to be skinned alive because we are not going to be caught. I have been working on the gang-leader at the quarry. When his men fill the passage they will leave a tunnel all the way down the top left-hand edge.'

'So, we don't open the door, we just crack off the top left corner – the one Dalifa put back with plaster … and climb through,' Paneb whispered.

'Almost,' Antef said. He leaned forward and spoke very softly as if the shadow of General Menes was listening. 'That corner is not very big. Too small for a fat lady like Maiarch or a heavy man like Neria. And I am too old and stiff to go crawling through holes. No, we will let you two young ones use that gap. You will hand out the valuables to us outside.'

'The guards will see us crawl in,' Dalifa argued. 'That was always a weakness in your plan, you know.'

Antef spread his hands. 'I am not the world's greatest thief for nothing. You see, I have already thought of this. I love you all dearly and I trust you all with my life ... but I couldn't tell you the most cunning part of my plot. If one of you had been caught and tortured the whole thing would have been ruined.'

The old man's face was lit by the orange palm-oil flame close to his face. His voice was now so soft his breath didn't even stir the flame. 'It is the part that will fool even clever General Menes.'

'There will be a tunnel to the broken corner of the door?' Dalifa said.

Antef nodded.

'We will go in, gather the treasures and drag them out?'

Antef's eyes just glimmered in answer.

'And no one will see us go in?' Paneb said.

'No one.'

'That's impossible,' Dalifa snorted.

'I am the world's greatest thief because I can do the impossible.' Antef sighed. 'It's an ancient trick I learned when I was Paneb's age and I worked with a magician. You open a box and pull out a dove. Yet no one saw you put the dove into the box.'

'Make sense, Antef,' Dalifa snapped. 'I don't believe in magic.'

'No one saw the magician put the dove in the box because ... the dove was already there. Simple. We put the dove in before we went on the stage.'

Dalifa gave a soft gasp. 'I see. Oh, that *is* clever, Antef. Very clever.'

'I don't see,' Paneb frowned.

'You will *not* climb down the tunnel into the tomb, Twig-boy. When Tutankhamun is buried you two will *already be* in the tomb! We will hide you there in the farthest corner. The funeral will finish. The door will close. The passage will be filled almost to the top. The tunnel is not there for you to get *in*. It is there for you to get out!'

Paneb swallowed hard. 'You want me to go into the King's tomb? In the dark? With his corpse?'

'You will have Dalifa with you. And think of the riches waiting for you outside,' Antef breathed.

But all the boy could think of was the horror. He knew that he wouldn't sleep that night.

***

They would spend the night on Antef's floor so they were ready to set off at first light.

Dalifa smiled at Paneb and said, 'I have seen those riches, Paneb. I made models of servants that will be buried with the King,' she said proudly.

'So they can serve him in the afterlife,' Paneb confirmed.

'One servant for each day of the year and enough jewellery to break a camel's back,' she went on.

'So how will we get it all out?' Paneb asked.

'One piece at a time,' Antef said. 'In these chambers there are some things far too heavy to carry out. You must break into the caskets and the shrines and steal as much as you can carry. Neria and I will be waiting at the end of the tunnel to carry it all to the boat.'

'I wondered why you let such a stupid man join us,' Dalifa said, nodding.

'He is a coffin-carrier. He will be dressed like one of the king's guards. We will make sure he is given the job of tomb guard.'

'But tell me about the afternoon – before we go in,' Paneb asked.

'Tomorrow afternoon the funeral will cross the Nile with the coffin and a lot of the treasures. They will stop at the entrance to the tomb and perform the opening of Tutankhamun's mouth.'

'That's so he will be able to see and hear and move in the next life,' Dalifa said.

'I know that,' Paneb told her.

'The King will be placed in his coffins – he has three of them – then the doors of his shrines will be closed. The King's food will be set out for him and the treasures arranged. Then the priests will sweep the floor and leave. They will close the door to the tomb and seal it.'

Dalifa explained, 'You are the head scribe. You can go in at noon – say you have to finish the last of the prayers. You've been there every day. The guards won't ask questions. You hide in the farthest corner. And I will take the last of the statues in a little while after you,' Dalifa said.

Antef sighed, 'They would question a girl carrying treasures out of the tomb. But they won't stop a girl carrying treasures in. It's a brilliant plan. It will work.'

'It *will* work,' Antef and Dalifa crowed and their laughter echoed off the walls like the cackle of a jackal.

DALIFA, DUST AND DOOM

Funeral day dawned. The Fabulous Five Thebes Thieves were ready after all the weeks of planning.

That is VERY difficult to say aloud without your false teeth falling out. So don't try it.

They checked their water-clocks for the last time in the light of the palm-oil lamps. As the sun began to rise over the desert they slipped out of the house. The streets of Thebes were bustling already. People had come from all over Egypt for the funeral and the city was swarming like an ants' nest.

... but with people, not ants ... and the swarming people had two legs where ants have six ... and they didn't live in nests, of course. So really Thebes was swarming only very loosely like an ants' nest.

There were dancers and beggars, fortune-tellers and jugglers setting up on the road through Thebes. There were also robbers and tricksters. But none of the robbers had as great a plan as the Fabulous Five.

Big Neria strode off to the House of Death. He was used to the smell now. Today it was bad because perfumes had been scattered over the coffin. Somehow the smell of scent and death was more sickly than death alone.

Tutankhamun's corpse had been gutted and dried and wrapped and it was now in its first coffin. Other corpses in the House of Death lay around for the flies to feast on. Today only the King mattered.

The Priest of Anubis strutted around giving orders. Even his jug-handle ears were dripping sweat. 'We leave when the sun reaches noon,' he said. 'Now let us get our procession sorted out. We must practise.'

'Why?' the fat guard, Thekel, asked.

'Because I don't want any accidents. I don't want idiots like you tripping up and dropping Tutankhamun in the dust,' the priest said and began to rage. 'The gods would be very angry. And so I would have to get angry because the gods act through me. And I would make sure the next corpse to fall in the dust would be yours, Thekel! Now pick up this practice coffin and let's try walking around the House of Death, shall we?'

Thekel stumbled several times and it was only Big Neria's strength that stopped the coffin crashing down. But by late morning they were just about perfect. The King's coffin was carried to a wooden sledge and Neria was one of the guards chosen to pull it.

The priests arrived from the Temple of Amun and Maiarch was among them. She was hot and weary from the walk, but excited. Neria waved at her but Maiarch shook her head. 'Don't let them see we know each other,' she mumbled quickly as she walked past the big man. 'We don't want any awkward questions.'

She took her place beside the other priests and priestesses.

The road across the desert was filling with people. Women in black started wailing and throwing road dust over their heads.

There was an argument between the Priest of Amun and the Priest of Anubis about who should walk at the head of the funeral.

Maiarch had seen a lot of life. She stepped between the two priests and said, 'My lords, I think the King would be mightily honoured if you both walked ahead of the coffin ... side by side. What King has ever had two great priests escort him to his grave?'

The Priest of Amun stretched his vulture neck with pride. 'You are right, Maiarch.'

The sweaty Priest of Anubis blew out his cheeks. 'I was going to suggest it myself!'

'Hah!' the Priest of Amun jeered. 'You were not!'

'Are you calling me a liar?' Anubis raged. 'If I didn't have this jackal head on I'd smack my forehead straight into your beaky nose!'

'So take the head off and let's see you try!' Amun barked.

As the priest reached for the jackal mask, Maiarch stepped between them again. 'My lords ... look!'

'What?'

'The sun has reached noon. The Queen will be waiting at the palace to join the procession. We don't want to keep her and the new King waiting. King Ay may be angry.'

The priests nodded. They arranged their robes and stood in front of the coffin. 'And it's not just the King and Queen who are waiting,' Maiarch muttered to herself. 'We can't keep little Paneb waiting too long either.'

The procession set off towards the city. Maiarch screamed, 'Aieeee!' and the other women joined her in the wailing that always went with a king's funeral. Some women picked up the dust from the road and threw it over themselves – but Maiarch was too stiff to bend down that low. Some women tore out lumps of hair – Maiarch wasn't going to do that either.

'I'm paid to wail so I'll wail. Aieeee!' she cried. She may not have thrown dust or torn hair but she wailed better than any of them. She was the princess of wails.

Princess of Wales ... princess of wails ... geddit? All right. That is the worst joke in the whole book and the last joke in the book (unless I can think of another one).

***

WAIL!
WAIL!
WAIL!
WAIL!
WAIL!
WAIL!
WAIL!
WHAT A DRAG!

When the sun reached noon Paneb left the scribe school and walked steadily towards the river. He carried his reed brushes and pots of paint.

A huge barge covered in gold-leaf and hung with a rainbow of silks sat at the quay on the east bank of the river. The funeral would arrive here halfway through noon and Tutankhamun would be carried over the Nile for his last journey. Paneb would be there before the body.

A hundred other boats paddled busily back and forth across the river. Paneb joined the queue with other tomb-workers and climbed aboard a ferry. They landed on the west bank and walked past the mighty temples on the road to the Valley of the Kings.

The guard stood in front of the entrance to the tunnel.

'Hello, Paneb,' he said.

'Hello, Henku,' the boy said with a nervous smile. If Henku refused to let him pass then the weeks of planning were ruined.

'I thought you'd be finished,' the guard said.

'No. The King will be put inside his outside coffin,' Paneb explained. That was true. 'Then it is sealed and I have to paint a final prayer across the seal.' That was a lie ... but it was a good lie.

'Ooooh!' I hear you cry. 'How can a lie be good? My teachers have always taught me lying is wicked.' All right, I'll explain. When I say it was a 'good' lie I mean it was a lie that would work. A 'bad lie' is, 'Please, sir, my dog ate my homework.' Nobody believes that old story any longer. Hopeless. Useless. A 'bad' lie. See?

Henku shrugged and said, 'I didn't know that.'

'Not a lot of people do,' Paneb said and walked on towards the tunnel that led to the tomb. The tomb had been cut into the rock of the cliff. The stone that had been taken out would be put back in once Tutankhamun was buried.

'And I am buried with him,' Paneb thought.

He walked into the tunnel and through the open door – the door with the cracked corner. Paneb knew he could break off the corner. But what if the tunnel was filled to the top? He would die slowly and be trapped forever.

The boy entered the tomb where craftsmen were laying out the things the King would need in the next life. Treasure chests and the jewelled models of servants that hairy little Kheperu was fussing over.

There was even a golden chariot in pieces on the floor. Tutankhamun and the gods would have to put it together if it was going to be any use in the afterlife.

Paneb took out his paint-pots and began work on a wall painting he had left unfinished. No one took any notice of him – they were all too busy looking after their own tasks.

One by one the craftsmen left and Paneb made his way to the room farthest from the door. A large treasure chest was close to the wall but there was just enough room for Paneb to squeeze in the space behind it.

A few lamps were left burning so the priests could see their way when they placed Tutankhamun in the stone coffins that stood in the main room. The tomb went silent ... so quiet Paneb could hear the blood racing through his head.

Then he heard the soft scuff of a sandal. The steps came closer to the door of the room where he was hiding.

A voice spoke softly. It said, 'Paneb!'

***

In the Royal Palace of Thebes, Queen Ankhesenamun sat pale and still as a statue in the temple. General Menes marched into the throne room in his finest uniform and saluted her. 'Hail, Majesty,' he cried.

The young Queen didn't move. The General lowered his voice. 'Hail, Majesty. The royal funeral has left the House of Death. They will be passing here soon and we will join the funeral procession.'

Ankhesenamun's beautiful eyes flickered a little and she spoke as softly as the flies that buzzed around the perfume in her hair. 'Yes.'

'Would you like me to arrange a chair to carry you?' the General asked, frowning and worried.

She shook her head. 'No. I will walk. The people expect it.' Suddenly tears sprang to her eyes. Tears that had been held back like water in a dam for ten weeks. 'He was only nineteen years old. Nineteen. We had so little time together!'

Menes was not used to comforting grieving women. He shuffled his feet. 'He is a god. He had just nineteen years on earth but he has the rest of time in a better place.'

'I want him here. I want him now,' Ankhesenamun groaned.

'You will join him one day,' Menes promised.

'I wish it was today.' The queen sighed, rose to her feet and smiled at the General. 'Sorry, Menes. You have a lot to worry about. You do not want to listen to my misery.'

Menes gave a small shrug. 'I have one thing less to worry about,' he said. 'I do not have to worry about the grave-robbers. I know their plans. This time tomorrow they will wish they had never been born!'

***

The funeral had reached the east bank of the Nile. King Ay had met the priests and led the procession down to the river. Maiarch watched as he ordered the coffin to be placed on the fine barge of gold and silk. Then Ay stepped aboard.

Queen Ankhesenamun followed in a smaller barge with General Menes by her side. Maiarch managed to join the queen's barge along with some of the other wailing, dust-covered women.

Maiarch turned to the woman next to her and mumbled, 'A cruel face, King Ay. It's easy to believe he had a hand in Tutankhamun's death, they way the gossips say.'

'That's dangerous talk,' the woman hissed. 'Stealing King Ay's good name could get you killed.'

Maiarch chuckled. 'There are more dangerous things in this life. Stealing a king's gold for a start!'

The barge slipped into the river and the women gave the wailing a rest for a while. The priests used reed rattles to make a soft sound that was meant to please the gods.

Maiarch's feet ached and she still had the walk from the west bank to the Valley of the Kings. But it would be worth it. Once she was a rich woman, she would never need to walk again.

***

Dalifa had hidden the carved stone model carefully. She'd stolen it from Kheperu's workshop one night and taken it home.

Now it was inside her tunic, held in place by a belt as she hurried towards the Valley of the Kings.

She sat on the hillside above the cave and watched as craftsmen hurried in and out. She could see the long funeral procession winding its way through the valley. The craftsmen began to leave the tomb and she spotted Kheperu the jeweller coming out, blinking into the sunlight.

'About time,' she muttered. 'I thought you'd never leave.'

He didn't see her. Just as well. Dalifa walked down the hillside. When she reached the new tomb she pulled the model servant out and waved it at the guard, Henku.

'What do you want?' the guard demanded.

Dalifa gave him her warmest smile and waved the statue. 'Look at this!'

'It's a doll.'

'It's a *model* of a servant for Tutankhamun,' she explained. 'He needs three hundred and sixty-five – one for every day of the year. Would you believe it? My master Kheperu only put in three hundred and sixty-four? Our poor King would be left without a servant for one day each year. How on earth would he manage?'

'I don't know...'

'So it's just as well I managed to make this last one in

time before the funeral arrives. I'll just slip it in the tomb with the others, if that's all right?'

'I suppose…'

'Thanks!' she said brightly.

'I'll have to search you when you come out,' Henku said.

'I don't mind,' Dalifa smiled. 'But you'd better get back on guard. That dust cloud means the funeral's getting closer.'

Henku hurried back to his post while Dalifa walked into the tunnel. She passed the door that she and Paneb had cracked and went into the farthest room.

***

Nepher could have been dead. The gang-leader from the tombs wasn't moving.

He was tied to a post in a dark room in a distant tower of the palace. His skin had been shredded by sharp knives. Nicked and peeled off his bones. Flies buzzed around the wounds and fed on the drying blood.

He wore only a loincloth. His head was sunk on to his blood-soaked chest. In the darkness a man's voice whispered, 'Nepher?'

The man gave a soft moan. 'Nepher? It's me. Weni!'

Nepher opened his eyes and tried to smile. 'Weni. My old friend. You must go. The guards ... they will find you and torture you the way Menes tortured me.'

Weni was a small man but with muscles like a desert lion. He moved behind the post and began to untie the ropes. 'No guards,' he murmured. 'Every guard in the palace is needed at the funeral.'

The rope came loose and Nepher began to fall forward. Weni moved quickly to catch him and sit him on the stone floor. Nepher groaned.

'I know,' little Weni soothed. 'It hurts.'

'No,' Nepher said. 'It's not that. Listen, Weni ... I agreed to help Antef the grave-robber.'

Weni nodded. 'I know.'

'Menes knew too. So he brought me here and started peeling strips of skin off me to make me talk.'

'I can see.'

'But I didn't talk. Not at first. I bled and suffered but I didn't talk.'

'I can see how much you suffered.'

'We are common people working together against the lords and the kings, their soldiers and their priests. Ordinary men and women against the rulers who hate us and need us,' Nepher whispered.

'You always told us that – the workers are with you, Nepher.'

'But in the end I cried out the plan. Oh, Weni ... I betrayed Antef and his friends. They think they are going to do the greatest robbery in history ... but I know they will be caught! What a traitor I am.'

Weni held out a ladle of water for his gang-master to drink. 'Maybe it's not too late. Maybe I can warn Antef?'

Nepher managed a smile. 'No, Weni. That is my job. What time is it?'

'Just after noon.'

'Then we have time. With your help I will warn Antef. Help me, Weni. You and me. We'll beat Menes. We are common people working together against the lords and the kings, their soldiers and their priests.'

Weni wept silently and did what Nepher told him.

***

'Paneb,' Dalifa said.

'Yes,' the boy whispered from his hiding place.

'Are you there?'

His wide eyes peered over the top of the treasure chest.

'You'd better hide here,' he said, squeezing himself into the corner.

'Not long now,' Dalifa said.

'Not long? We'll be here all night and most of tomorrow,' Paneb said.

'Hah!' Dalifa laughed. 'And if we can't find our way out we'll be here a lot longer than that. Think of it ... buried alive. Heh! Heh!'

'It's not funny,' Paneb squeaked.

'Hush. I hear them outside.'

***

The sun was sinking by the time the funeral reached the entrance to the tomb. The lords and priests chanted, 'O King! Come in peace! O God! Protector of the Land!' then the Priest of Amun opened the mummy's mouth so his spirit could escape.

The coffin was lifted off the sledge and Neria helped to carry it down the sloping tunnel into the tomb. Maiarch waddled after her High Priest of Amun and no one noticed. While the priests saw to the coffins, Maiarch slipped round a corner into the treasure room.

She had carried a bundle wrapped around her waist. She was so chubby no one noticed the extra roll. Maiarch unwound it and placed it on the treasure chest. She whispered, 'There you are, my children, food and beer, a water-clock, a hammer and a chisel. I'll see you tomorrow.'

The old woman didn't wait for a reply. She walked past the door to the coffin room. Tutankhamun's widow was saying her last farewell with flowers. She laid olive leaves, blue water-lily petals and cornflowers on the coffin. The Queen sobbed and was led out of the door of the tomb.

Maiarch joined the priests just before they closed the door. It slid into place with a *boom*.

To Dalifa and Paneb, trapped inside, it sounded more like *doom*.

WATER, WOE AND WORK

Antef was worried. The workers had begun filling in the corridor that led to the entrance door of the tomb. He hurried over to a labourer. 'Where is your gang-leader, Nepher?' he asked.

The labourer shrugged. 'Haven't seen him for two days. His old friend Weni has gone to look for him.'

Antef licked his parched lips. He swallowed hard and took a risk. 'Did Nepher tell you how to fill the tunnel?' he asked.

The labourer looked up at the guard, Henku, who stood above the entrance to the cave, watching them.

'We know how to fill the tunnel. We leave a narrow hole at the top left corner all the way to the door. Wide enough for a boy to crawl through.'

Antef nodded and slapped the labourer's shoulder. 'Good man.'

'But,' the labourer warned, 'if Henku up there checks he may notice ... he may order us to fill the whole corridor. Then what will you do?'

'Leave Henku to me,' Antef murmured.

The labourer leaned on his shovel. 'I've opened graves where robbers were trapped inside. Opened them too late. Their fingers were raw and their nails splintered where they'd tried to claw their way out. But the air goes stale and they choke on their own breath. It's an ugly way to die.'

Antef thought of Paneb and Dalifa inside the tomb. They could live for a week on the food and beer Maiarch had left them. But they could only live two days on the air trapped inside.

'Fill it as Nepher told you,' he said. 'Henku will not be here to check your work.'

'You're sure?'

'I'm sure.'

***

Paneb and Dalifa set the water-clock. When it was emptied, filled and emptied again they knew it would be time to leave. They wandered through the tomb and gathered all the treasures that could be carried through the narrow gap they'd make.

Golden ornaments were bundled into cloths and left ready at the door. It was cool in the chamber, not cold. But Paneb shivered. Gods and ghosts were haunting him. He'd have sworn they were there in the shadows.

Dalifa handed Paneb golden armbands and statues, jewels and rings. He scrabbled in the wooden cases and came up with more. Soon they had twenty small bags packed tight with treasures. Ten journeys ... if they could get out.

The two thieves heard the workmen piling stones against the door. They knew it was night. They knew the work would be finished some time in the early morning.

They prayed that Antef had picked the right gang to bribe.

They ate and drank a little outside the door of the coffin room.

'I'm a princess, you know, Paneb,' Dalifa said.

'Really,' Paneb replied. His voice was flat. He didn't believe her but he didn't dare tell her he didn't believe her.

'One day I will be buried like this,' she said.

'Ah.' The boy nodded. He sat on the floor and rested his head against one of the walls he'd painted.

'And as a princess I really should be marrying a king – or a lord of Egypt at least,' Dalifa said and sat beside him.

'Hm.'

'When I am rich – and have a fine house and servants – the lords will queue at my door to marry me.'

'Mmm.'

'But if you wanted to join the queue, Paneb ... I mean, I know you're not a lord ... but after tonight you'll be very rich ... what I'm saying is ... I might let you stand at the front of the queue. Even though you're a peasant. I'll tell you a secret ... but you have to promise not to tell anyone. Promise? You see ... you know that story about me being a princess? Well ... Antef and Kheperu think it's my little fantasy. The story about me making statues in the city of Tyre is a dream. I know they laugh at me. It ... it just happens to be true! So what do you think of that, Paneb, my dear Twig-boy?'

She turned and peered at him in the weak light of the lamp. But Paneb was sleeping and snoring softly.

'Oh.' Dalifa sighed. She gently placed one of the King's robes over him. It covered her too.

She eventually fell asleep.

***

Nepher's wounds were wrapped tightly in bandages. He was a strong man and a brave one. With Weni's help he shuffled down to the east bank of the river. A fisherman helped lift the gang-leader into his boat and didn't ask about his wounds or why he wanted to travel to the Valley of the Kings. But Weni explained.

'Nepher is the gang-leader with the job of filling the tunnel to the tomb. He had an accident but he is determined to see the job completed.'

The fisherman nodded and paddled towards the setting sun.

Barges from the funeral were coming back now. Women who had wailed on the way there were chatting and laughing. Priests who had preened and paraded in their pomp at the tomb now kicked off their sandals and let servants wash their dusty feet.

Guards who had stood rigid for hours now slumped in the boats with their beer.

On the west bank Menes stood with Queen Ankhesenamun. 'You must cross the river before dark, Your Majesty,' Menes fretted.

The Queen stared over the dark water at the happy funeral party. 'I cannot leave my husband,' she said looking back down the road to the Valley of the Kings.

'King Ay will be your husband tomorrow,' Menes reminded her. 'He'll be waiting for you.'

'Then let's leave.' Ankhesenamun sighed as softly as a crocodile ripple in the water.

'No!' Menes said sharply.

'No?'

'Sorry, Your Majesty, I didn't mean to shout. But I have business on this side of the river.'

'Business?'

'Tomb-robbers,' Menes said.

'You have guards,' Ankhesenamen told him.

'I have left Henku there to oversee the workers,' Menes said. 'But...'

'Your first duty is to see me safely back to the palace,' the Queen said sharply. 'Leave tomb-robbers to the eye of Horus.'

General Menes chewed his lip and followed his Queen to the royal barge. He watched a small fishing boat land on the shore. A man in bandages stumbled on to the land. Menes watched the figure limp painfully and slowly along the road to the Valley of the Kings. 'Sailors,' he cried to the crew of the Queen's barge. 'Get us across as quickly as you can!'

The barge set off.

***

Antef was more weary than he had ever been in his life. He was so close to his great dream. Now he had to make one last effort. It was as if he'd climbed a mountain. He was almost at the top but was too tired to make the last few steps.

He breathed in the cool evening air. He fixed a smile on his face and slapped Big Neria on the shoulder. 'Let's go,' he said cheerfully.

The opening to the tomb was filled with workers

scurrying back and forth with sledges full of loose stones. The men sweated and worked quietly.

On a ledge above the entrance the guard Henku yawned and stretched.

Antef marched up to the man. 'Henku, my friend!'

'Your friend?'

'My dear friend.'

'Who are you?'

'You remember *me*? I'm old Bahari!' he said.

'Bahari's a village. Are you from there?'

'No ... it's just my name.'

'Ah.'

'I'm a servant at the palace,' Antef went on.

'Ah.'

'And I've brought a message from General Menes,' Antef lied, tapping a scroll tucked under his belt. He pulled it out and unrolled it. 'This is a list of guard duties.'

'Oh?'

'And you have been on guard here all afternoon ... all through the funeral ... because you're the best,' Antef explained.

Henku grinned. 'Does it say that on your scroll?'

'Yes, read it for yourself!'

'I can't read,' Henku said.

Antef had guessed that. 'It says ... most loyal Henku will guard the tomb until sunset...'

'Ohhhh! No!' Henku objected. 'General Menes said till sun*rise*.'

Antef shook his head and tapped the scroll. 'Sunset, it

says here.' The old man held out the scroll for Neria to look at. 'What does it say, Neria?'

'Sun*set*,' Neria replied ... even though he couldn't read either. He just repeated what Antef had told him. 'And it says ... "The mighty warrior Neria the Bold is to take the place of Henku."'

Henku nodded. 'In that case I'll just wait for this mighty warrior to turn up.'

'You're *speaking* to him!' Antef laughed.

'You? I thought you said your name was Bahari.'

'Did I? ... I mean ... I did. No, this is Neria the Bold!' he said slapping the bare arm of the Fabulous Five Thief at his side.

'See?' Neria said. 'I have the King's seal on my belt.'

'You have,' Henku agreed.

'I'm not a thief trying to pretend that I'm a guard just so we get you out of the way and rob the tomb!' Neria laughed.

'Aren't you?'

'No, no-o,' Neria went on. 'I'm not a tomb-robber ... at least I've never robbed a tomb in my life before tonight.'

'Before tonight?'

Antef cut in quickly, 'He means he's a loyal servant of the King and he will guard the tomb with his life.'

'And I'm not a tomb-robber. Honest. I'm not! I'm really, really not. You believe me, don't you?'

Henku scowled. 'Why would I not believe you?'

''Cos ... 'cos...'

'Shut up, Neria,' Antef groaned. 'Just take your club

and stand guard. Look, the workers have nearly finished filling in the tomb.'

'Except for that top corner,' Henku pointed out.

'We'll make sure they do that. Now you hurry home before it gets dark and you trip over a crocodile in the dark ... or step on a scorpion ... or get eaten by a desert lion.'

Henku shuddered and said, 'I'm off.'

Antef watched him disappear into the gloom and rubbed his hands. 'Almost there, friend Neria. Almost there.'

Night fell and the weaker eye of Horus lit the sky.

***

Menes's face was dark and angry as a stormy sky. He hurried the Queen's servants along. They carried her on the chair and they sped up the east shore towards the palace in Thebes. 'The Queen is tired. Hurry. She needs to get to her bed. Hurry!'

'If we go any faster we'll drop her,' one of the carriers grumbled, but they jogged along and scattered cats through the streets of Thebes.

Please note, the publishers wish to make it clear, no cats were hurt in the making of this book. No dogs, camels, scorpions or dung beetles either if you are really worried.

When Menes had seen the Queen safely through the gates of the palace he marched quickly down to the kitchens. He snatched some bread and wine and swallowed the meal quickly.

Then he went to the guardhouse and armed himself with a knife and a heavy club. Before he left he had to climb the stairs to the tower to check if his prisoner Nepher had died yet. The guards could throw the body into the river tomorrow morning. The crocodiles could feast on human flesh. It would serve the man right.

The door wasn't locked. There was no need. Nepher had been tied to the post in the middle of the room. Menes wasted time finding an oil lamp and it lit his way into the room.

The post stood there. Ropes lay tangled on the floor.

Nepher was gone.

General Menes swore a thousand evil curses and ran from the palace towards the whispering Nile.

It was very thoughtful of the Nile to whisper. After all you wouldn't want it singing the latest songs, would you? Songs like 'I'll love you forever' ... or do I mean, 'Nile love you forever'? Whichever. A singing river would keep everyone awake. The Nile was far too thoughtful for that. It whispered.

The riverbank was deserted now. The boatmen had all gone home. Menes jumped into the nearest fishing boat and snatched at an oar. He jabbed the paddle into the river and hit something hard.

It was the skull of a skulking crocodile searching for its evening meal. The crocodile opened its huge jaws and snapped at the paddle. Then it crunched through the reed boat and sent the General tumbling into the River Nile.

Menes drew his knife and threw himself at the thrashing monster.

***

Nepher had fainted. Weni had tried to carry him but he hadn't the strength. The gang-leader had made it past the towering temples and on towards the workers' village of Deir el-Medina. A labourer was carrying water home.

'Help me!' Weni begged.

The labourer helped carry Nepher into the house where his wife was nursing her children to sleep.

'This man is half dead,' she said.

'He has to reach the Valley of the Kings by sunrise,' Weni groaned. 'Lives depend on it.'

The woman went to a chest in the corner of the room and took out her ointments and potions. 'His wounds are opening and he's losing blood. He needs to rest. I need to bind the wounds in fresh bandages. He needs to drink some potions to bring his strength back.'

'Then please hurry,' Weni said.

Even the moon had set by the time the woman had finished swaddling Nepher in fresh bandages. 'Who did this?' she asked.

'General Menes,' Weni told her.

'No man should torture another like this.'

Nepher opened his eyes a little. 'Ordinary men and women against the rulers who hate us and need us,' he murmured. 'But we'll win in the end.'

'Rest now,' the woman said. 'It's too dark to travel. The moon has set and the strong eye of Horus hasn't risen.'

But Nepher was already asleep.

***

Inside the tomb Dalifa and Paneb woke. The water-clock said it was time to leave.

Dalifa turned to the door and began to scrape at a crack in the top corner with her dagger. The corner broke off, as Antef said it would, and there was just enough room for someone small like Paneb or Dalifa to crawl through.

They felt cool morning air blow in to greet them. They knew a corner of the tunnel was open.

'Time to go!' Dalifa said.

Paneb jumped up the tunnel within the passage. The girl passed one of the bags to him. He hauled himself into the dark hole and crawled along. It was easier than breaking into a house but the stones scraped at his knees and elbows. He had to move very slowly or he'd be a shredded and bloody mess after ten journeys like this.

He could hear Dalifa behind him, gasping and dragging more treasure up the tunnel. He stopped and Dalifa's head hit the soles of his feet. 'Hurry, Twig-boy,' she hissed.

'No need to hurry,' he called back. 'We need to save our strength. We've ten journeys each to make. If the others are out there we are safe.'

'And if they're not?' Dalifa asked.

That was the question Paneb didn't want to think about. What if Antef had been arrested? What if the Valley was filled with guards waiting to carry them off to execution? What would it feel like to be crucified on the walls of Thebes?

He shuffled on.

He finally felt the cool morning air on his face and blinked into the early light.

Big Neria stood there, looking pleased. He had a sledge to load the treasure on – the same sledge that had carried Tutankhamun's body to the tomb.

Antef was there. He pulled open the first treasure bag, eyes alight with the morning sun. Maiarch stretched out a hand to help Dalifa with the other bag of treasure.

The women hugged one another and Maiarch even let tears roll down her cheeks. 'Well done, Dalifa!'

Paneb breathed hard. He brushed the stone chips off his scratched legs. Antef smiled at him. 'You did well, boy. You deserve to be rich.'

'It was your plan, Antef. We couldn't have done it without you.'

Then Big Neria came out with one of those wise sayings that he sometimes did. 'We haven't got away with it yet!'

And Paneb shivered. The sky was slate grey. The strong eye of Horus would be fully risen soon. Watching. Spying. And if Horus didn't see them then a passing peasant might. Paneb scrambled back into the tunnel and heard Dalifa cry, 'Wait for me!'

***

The battle had been long and bloody. The crocodile lay dead on the east bank of the Nile and General Menes lay beside it.

Even the guard's bronze muscles had been tired out by the struggle. His club had floated away down the Nile and his knife was snapped off somewhere in the skull of the crocodile.

Oh, all right, no crocodiles were hurt either in the making of this tale. Crocodiles have been hurt in the making of shoes and handbags but NOT for this book. I do not want to have to say this again so stop fretting.

The General's uniform was as shredded as his skin. He lay for a long while and gathered his strength.

At last he pushed himself up on to his feet and swayed. He staggered towards another reed boat. This time there was enough light in the sky for him to see the water was clear of creeping crocodiles before he planted the boat in the water and pushed off.

***

Queen Ankhesenamun couldn't sleep. Her maids brought her wine with soothing herbs. It only made her more awake. 'Bring me a plain robe,' she ordered.

She dressed quickly and went in search of General Menes.

A sleepy guard said the General had gone to the river at nightfall. He should be back at the Valley of the Kings by now. Ankhesenamun ordered the guard to follow her to the river.

The two found a small barge and the Queen told the guard to row her across to the west bank.

Ahead of them was a man paddling steadily. He could have been General Menes, Ankhesenamun thought. But he should have been far ahead of her by now. Anyway the man was in a tattered tunic and it seemed to be stained with red. He jumped ashore and vanished along the road past the temples.

Ankhesenamun urged her guard to row faster as the man struggled.

The strong eye of Horus was lighting the top of Mount Qurn when she stepped ashore.

***

Nepher awoke as the sun struck the top of Mount Qurn. The woman gave him food and beer and he managed to rise to his feet. Resting his arm around Weni's shoulder he limped along the last stretch of road to the Valley of the Kings. 'This way,' Nepher gasped as they reached a fork in the road. 'It brings us out on to the ledge above the tomb. We'll be able to see if there are any guards around.'

Weni guided and half carried the moaning man along the path. They reached the final turn in the Valley and saw the Fabulous Five Thieves working at the grave of Tutankhamun. 'Leave me now, Weni,' Nepher said. 'If Menes gets here soon then everyone will die. There is no need for you to risk your life. Leave me. Go back to your wife.'

Weni wanted to argue but he knew Nepher was right.

He watched Nepher walk slowly down the path that ended above the tomb entrance.

If he'd looked over his shoulder he'd have seen another bleeding man limping along a hundred beats of the water-clock behind them.

***

Inside the tomb Paneb gathered the second bag of treasure and threw it into the tunnel. Dalifa had opened her bag and was letting the oil lamp glint on the treasure. 'Wonderful things,' she sighed. 'Fit for a princess! I am sure Antef will let me keep some of these jewels for myself. To make me beautiful.'

The amber light shone on her face – a face without the eye colour and the cheek paint. It made her skin glow like gold and her eyes sparkle like lapis stones.

'You don't need jewels to make you beautiful,' Paneb muttered.

Dalifa's mouth fell open. 'What did you say?' she gasped. But Paneb was gone. The girl followed him and dragged her treasure after her. Her leading hand snatched at his ankle. 'What did you say, Paneb?'

He kicked himself free. 'Nothing.'

'You did!' she cried and giggled. 'You said I was beautiful.'

'I didn't,' he argued and wriggled faster.

'You did!'

'Didn't!' he called back and her fingers tickled the soles of his feet. Paneb had spent his life a thief. He'd never played before. Suddenly he was enjoying himself. He laughed and heard Dalifa laugh behind him.

'Wait till I get you!' she sniggered.

'I'd rather be got by General Menes!' Paneb groaned. He staggered out of the hole and turned to pull Dalifa after him. As he did so Maiarch looked past him and she clutched a fat hand to her open, pink-gummed mouth.

Something flickered in the corner of Paneb's eye. Something white. He turned and looked above the entrance to the tomb.

'The mummy!' Maiarch screamed. 'Tutankhamun has risen from the dead!' The old woman fell to her knees. Antef and Neria slowly dropped beside her and began to pray. 'Tutankhamun!' Maiarch screeched. 'He has come to avenge himself! Aieeee! Forgive us, lord! Forgive us!' The white figure in bandages staggered forward and lurched towards Paneb. It fell into the boy's frozen arms...

***

Paneb was too frightened to speak. The mummy was warm in his arms and its hand slowly moved up to its bandaged face. It tugged at the bandage and pulled it away from its mouth.

Then the mummy spoke. 'Antef!' it groaned.

'That's me, master. I'm sorry ... I wasn't robbing your grave, lord. I was just borrowing a few things ... forgive me ... we were going to put them back...' the old thief babbled.

'Antef,' the mummy cried. 'Friend. We are ordinary

men and women against the rulers. I didn't mean to betray you. Forgive me.'

Antef moved towards the bandaged figure and looked into its eyes. 'Nepher?'

The old man gently took his bandaged friend from Paneb and held him. 'What have they done to you?'

Nepher shook his head. 'It was Menes. But listen, Antef. He tortured me till I told him the plan. Menes knows. He must be on his way. He'll have a hundred men of the palace guard with him. You have to flee. Save yourself.'

Antef turned to the others. 'Put the loot on the sledge and then put Nepher on top. We'll drag him back to the village. The workers will hide him and care for him till he's well again. The poor look after one another.'

Big Neria lifted Nepher gently and easily on to the sledge. Neria heaved on the rope and began to drag it along.

He hadn't moved the length of a man's foot before a voice boomed, 'Stop!'

Paneb groaned as he looked around and saw General Menes standing at the mouth of the tomb. The General was torn and wounded but still as frightening as ever.

'He has no weapon!' Neria cried and raised his knife. 'Shall I kill him, Antef?'

'We are thieves, not murderers,' Antef said bitterly. 'Lords like Ay can murder King Tutankhamun and be rewarded with his crown. But if we harmed Menes we'd be hunted like fish and murdered.'

'And die very slowly,' Menes reminded him.

You wanted a happy ending? Sorry. This is based on a true story, remember. I can't just rewrite history so you can go around with a smile on your face. Of all the lessons of history, this is the horriblest. Remember: happy endings are for fairy tales. Horrible endings are usually history.

'Let the children go, Menes,' Antef said softly.

Menes snorted. 'We have been hunting the boy for years. He is the house-breaker and a plague on Thebes. He deserved to die even before this grave robbery. I will execute him first so you can watch,' the General promised.

'The girl,' Maiarch whined. 'At least you can spare the girl?'

General Menes shrugged. 'I will spare her life ... but she will spend the rest of that life as my slave.'

Dalifa smiled sweetly. 'I would rather die, thank you. Nail me to the walls of Thebes alongside Paneb and I will die happy.'

'I will drive in the nails myself,' Menes sneered. 'You will all die.'

'No one will die,' a soft voice behind Menes said.

***

A woman stood there. She wore a plain white gown and a luxurious wig. Her sweet perfume drifted down to Paneb. She was the most beautiful thing he'd ever seen in his young life.

And the most frightening. He felt sick with fear. His joy at crawling out with the riches had felt as sweet as honey – now his despair tasted like ashes.

His mouth fell open. Menes said, 'Don't you peasants kneel when you come before your queen, Ankhesenamun?'

The Fabulous Failed Five fell to their knees in front of Tutankhamun's widow.

'I will have sharp wooden stakes put up by the river,' the General said. 'I will have you thieves taken up the cliff path and dropped on to the stakes. They will be seen from the roads and the river so all of Thebes can see what happens to grave-robbers.' His eyes were as bright with the thought of their deaths as Antef's had been at the sight of treasure. 'It will take a day or so for you to die. You will scream, you will suffer agonies. Have you anything to say before I kill you?'

And Antef remembered the words of the workman at this tomb nine weeks before. He murmured, 'We are common people working together against the lords and the kings, their soldiers and their priests. Ordinary men and women against the rulers who hate us and need us. It's always been that way. It always will be.' He looked up and said to the Queen, 'We may as well die. We will never be free.'

The Queen looked up towards the eye of Horus. 'Free? You think I am free?'

'Yes, Your Majesty.'

Ankhesenamun laughed bitterly. 'My young husband Tutankhamun is dead. I am forced to marry his old uncle to make his power stronger. What sort of freedom is that? Only Tutankhamun is truly free. If I have you killed then you will be free too.'

'If?' General Menes snapped.

The Queen turned to him. 'No more deaths, Menes. My husband died for the treasures of Egypt. These poor people need not die.'

The joy slipped from the face of General Menes. 'They must be punished, Your Highness.'

The sad-faced Queen spread her hands. 'They hoped

to steal a life of laziness,' she sighed. 'So punish them with a life of work. Set them to work in the fields.'

The General shook his head. 'As you wish, Your Highness,' he spat.

She pointed to Nepher whose wounds were bleeding through his bandages. 'That man has suffered enough. He must go free.'

Antef managed a smile. 'You are a good lady. That is a just decision.'

Menes walked over to Neria and took his knife. He turned and held the knife at Antef's throat. 'To the river, you filthy little thief.' He looked at Paneb. 'And you, boy, can return the treasure to where you found it.' He pointed at Big Neria. 'Then you can start filling in that tunnel.'

Paneb went back down the tunnel. It seemed a long and hopeless journey. The last oil lamp was guttering on the floor. He placed the treasure carelessly back where he'd found it.

Then he opened the large linen bag. Inside he found one small silk bag. It was filled with thirty golden rings. Enough of a fortune to last the Fabulous Five for a year at least.

He tucked the bag of rings into his belt – Menes would never guess it was there. He set off through the tunnel again. Cruel rocks clawed at him and the rough roof scraped at his head. He didn't care.

When Paneb crawled out Queen Ankhesenamun had gone.

And so were the rings. They'd been pulled from his belt as he crawled along.

Neria started filling the tunnel.

Paneb said goodbye to his dreams.

***

By noon the next day the sun was high and even the crocodiles were too hot to move from the river. But the Fabulous Five were using shadufs to lift water from the Nile and working the fields, pulling at weeds till their backs were breaking and sweat flowed like the Nile.

Just yesterday, one day before, they had been dreaming of a life of ease and more riches than they could ever spend. One dreadful day later and they had only the nightmare of work and poverty.

The guards let them stop to drink a little weak beer and chew on an onion each. 'We were wrong to try and rob the dead, Antef,' Paneb moaned and sank to the ground beside the old man.

Antef looked at the boy quickly. 'No. We were not wrong. The only thing we did wrong was get caught. There was nothing wrong with trying to make ourselves rich.'

Paneb looked across the fields to the palace of Tutankhamun. 'But even the Queen doesn't look happy with all her riches,' he said.

Antef snorted. 'No. Today King Ay will marry little widow, Queen Ankhesenamun.'

'He's an old man,' Dalifa said. 'Poor lady. When I marry a lord he'll be young and handsome ... like Paneb.'

The boy blushed.

Antef looked up and slapped Paneb's aching shoulders with his horny hand. 'He is *old*! Hah! There's a thought, Paneb! King Ay is old!'

'So?' Paneb asked.

Antef's legs were aching but he managed a little dance in the mud of the fields. The guards raised their spears as if he had gone mad.

'He's old!' he laughed. 'You see?'

'Yes! He's *old*,' Dalifa giggled.

'So what?' Big Neria grunted and frowned.

'Old!' Maiarch crowed. 'Oh, yes, so very old. It's wonderful! He's old! He's old, he's OLD!'

'So?' Paneb cried. 'So what? I don't see why that would make you so happy.'

Antef waved a hand and gathered the other four thieves in a huddle where the guards wouldn't hear.

'So … he will *die* soon. And when he does, they will bury him with all his wealth. And another time we'll be more careful. Another time we'll make sure we aren't caught!'

A guard cracked a whip and ordered them back to the baked fields.

'Another time?'

Antef grinned his broken-toothed grin. 'Another time. Another day. A better day, Paneb. There will always be a better day.'

Goodness me. I think he may be right. An old saying goes, 'When things are at the worst they begin to get better.' Maybe it's not such a horrible ending after all.

The Fabulous Five of Thebes went back to their work laughing.

Epilogue

There is truth in this tale.

Tutankhamun's tomb was found again in 1922. A team of archaeologists went in and robbed it.

> **They did a better job than the tomb-robbers of old. They really cleaned it out.**

Tutankhamun's corpse and his fortune have been lugged around the world for people to stare at. Rest in eternal peace? No chance.

Some historians think Tut has a cracked skull and that he may have been murdered by his Uncle Ay.

The archaeologists discovered that the tomb had been robbed shortly after Tutankhamun was buried. There were probably TWO robberies at the time. Tomb-workers are the chief suspects.

The top corner of the door was cracked where the thieves had broken in. They must have dug a little tunnel along the top of the stones that filled the big tunnel.

The riches inside the tomb had been scattered by thieves in a hurry. The thieves had clearly been disturbed or caught because the tomb had been sealed up again and many valuables left behind. But one of the gangs got away with over half of Tut's jewels.

The clue to how the robbers got in was in the little tunnel. A bag of rings was found near the roof. Paneb's rings.

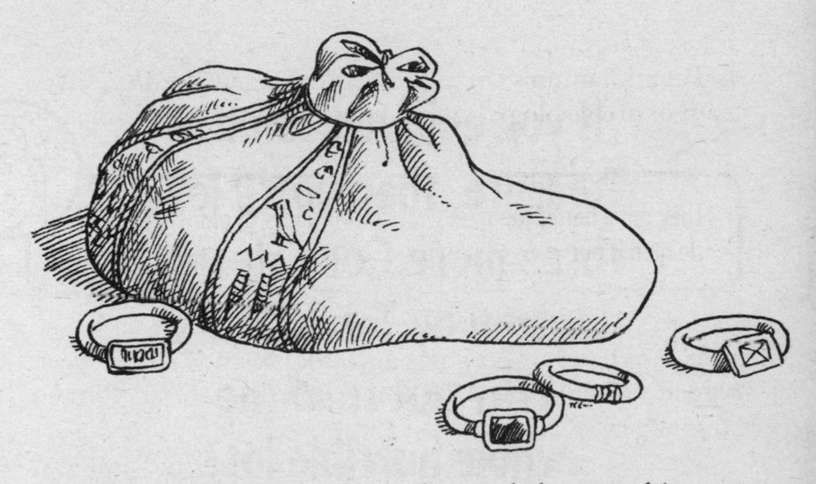

A grave-robber must have dropped them on his way out. When the gap had been filled in no one noticed the little bag.

If the robber knew he'd dropped the rings why didn't he go back? Because he was caught?

Poor robber. Saying goodbye to all his dreams.

If you enjoyed Tomb of Treasure, then you'll love three more Gory Stories, written by Terry Deary. Why not read the whole horrible lot?

A wild and wind-lashed wall separates two terrifying tribes: the Picts and the Britons. Two Gaul soldiers are given the task of guarding the wall – on pain of death. But with catapults, feasts and football to distract them, will they be able to keep the peace and solve the mystery of the lost legion?

Find out in this Rotten Roman adventure, it's got all the gore and so much more!

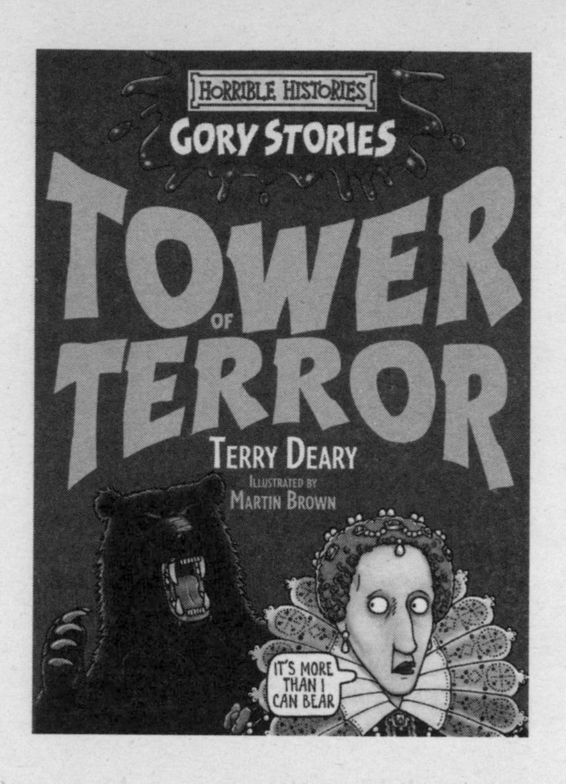

Simon Tuttle and his Pa are tricksters struggling to make a living on the Tudor streets. When disaster strikes Simon must fend for himself, even if it means committing treason. But can he pull off his Pa's carefully concocted plan and should he trust his mysterious new accomplice?

Find out in this Terrible Tudor adventure, it's got all the gore and so much more!

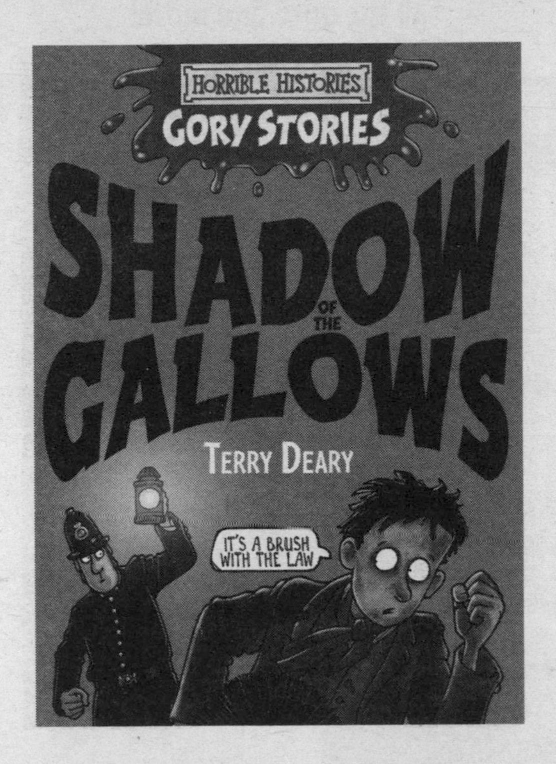

When a boy called Bairn is rescued from his dangerous job as an Edinburgh chimney sweep, he appears to have landed on his feet. But his new job proves just as dangerous and he soon becomes caught up in a plot to kill Queen Victoria. Has he been saved from slavery only to end up swinging at the gallows?

Find out in this Vile Victorian adventure, it's got all the gore and so much more!

Don't miss these horribly handy Handbooks for all the gore and more!

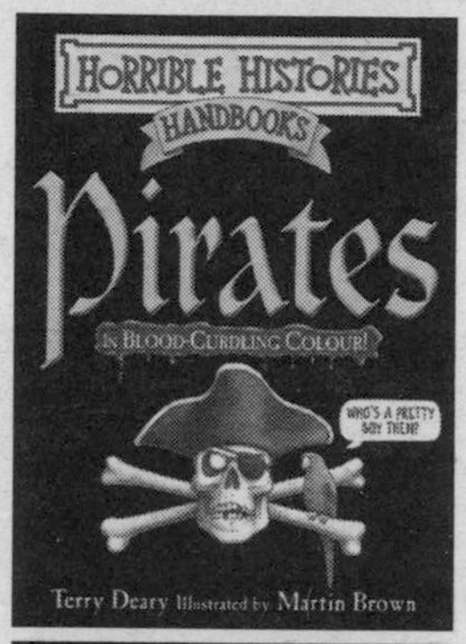

Terry Deary was born at a very early age, so long ago he can't remember. But his mother, who was there at the time, says he was born in Sunderland, north-east England, in 1946 – so it's not true that he writes all *Horrible Histories* from memory. At school he was a horrible child only interested in playing football and giving teachers a hard time. His history lessons were so boring and so badly taught, that he learned to loathe the subject. *Horrible Histories* is his revenge.

Martin Brown was born in Melbourne, on the proper side of the world. Ever since he can remember he's been drawing. His dad used to bring back huge sheets of paper from work and Martin would fill them with doodles and little figures. Then, quite suddenly, with food and water, he grew up, moved to the UK and found work doing what he's always wanted to do: drawing doodles and little figures.